The Last Unforgiven
CURSED

Demons, Book 4

By Marina Simcoe

To My Captain

Chapter 1

RAIM, THE GRAND MASTER of Western Council of Incubi, rose from his seat in the meeting room at the Base in Yukon. The old armchair groaned as if relieved to be free of his weight.

"The Council is yours, Stolas." He refused to address the demon by his human name, Andras. Instead, he preferred to call all Incubi by the names they received at the time of their creation, lest they forget who they were and where they came from.

"Lead it wisely," he added, not even attempting to hide a sarcastic smile.

As intelligent and resourceful as Stolas had proven to be, Raim doubted he had the necessary ruthlessness and ingenuity to balance Incubi's interests with The Priory's demands.

For a moment, Raim considered telling Stolas about the *soros* stone urn, the only one that survived the journey to this world intact and had been in the possession of The Priory for the past six hundred years. Then decided against it.

The Elder would no doubt let the new Grand Master know about the true source of human power over the Incubi. So far, Stolas and The Elder seemed to get along splendidly in their common goal to unite humans and demons.

A sting of resentment pierced through Raim. They all went against his own efforts to prevent the integration of the demons into the human society, crushing his control over his own kind.

He refused to remain their Grand Master on current terms.

Still, the centuries-old habit of looking after the interests of this ungrateful bunch of demons was hard to beat.

"Beware of the Priory," Raim couldn't hold back the warning before exiting the room. "They are the ones with the real power."

Not that it mattered anymore. Nothing did. Incubi were doomed from the moment Sytry broke the rule of silence and spoke to that Source last year.

"Where are you going?" Stolas called out behind him.

Raim didn't dignify him with an answer. Wasn't it enough that he was leaving the Council he had ruled most of his existence, giving up everything he had built and failed to preserve?

Stolas could have it all. Raim owed him nothing more.

The white silk of his robe streamed in the air behind him as he swiftly walked along the corridor, then up the stairs. Out of habit, he turned right at the top of the stairs but stopped, having taken just a couple of steps. There was nothing he needed from his room, not a thing he would miss if left behind.

Resolutely, he spun on his heel and headed to the exit instead.

The door at the Base had not been guarded for months now, and Raim walked out without having to say a word to anyone else.

Crossing the property towards a number of vehicles parked by the wall, he yanked free the jewelled clasp that held his robe closed at his shoulder, and tossed it into the snow. The wind caught the silk, his robe flew open, and he let it slide off his shoulders and flutter to the ground.

Left dressed only in a pair of black pants and a thin white tunic, Raim felt the winter chill seep through just one layer of cloth. The sensation felt invigorating as he climbed behind the wheel of a truck.

Fishing the keys out of the glove compartment, he started the engine and drove off the property where he had spent most of his time during the past few centuries.

His phone rang, and he yanked it out of his pocket. Without glancing at the screen to see who was calling, he rolled down the window and tossed the phone into the snowbank on the side of the road.

The Incubi had doomed themselves, rushing out there like a pack of eager puppies wagging their tails, to claim the first female who would allow them to come close enough.

Once tasted, the sweet energy of a human female was impossible to resist for his kind. It took over a demon's mind and soul like poison, eventually destroying both.

He didn't need to stay and watch as the Incubi whom he had tried so hard to protect learned the true, treacherous nature of a female heart. And they would fall, the way he had fallen—crushed, ruined, and destroyed for an eternity.

Driving along the snowy road, Raim rubbed his forehead, wincing at the painful memories that tortured him every hour of every century.

"God did not curse me with the centuries of torment, Olyena. *You* did."

Chapter 2

RAIM TOOK THE COVER off the gramophone he had on the side table in the spacious living room of his mansion in Switzerland, and set a vinyl disk with Beethoven Symphony number seven on it.

After several decades of owning the device, he still marvelled at human ingenuity as the sound of the orchestra filled the room.

Raim had heard the symphony performed live once. He knew this music was the result of the perfectly coordinated work of many people in conjunction with their instruments. Yet all of that was now compacted onto a black plastic disk that spun on the gramophone, a device that modern humans would already find extremely obsolete, even though he had it for less than a century.

Disposable.

That applied to human civilization as a whole. They wasted their genius and their short, fragile lives.

Suddenly, Raim felt the movement of air at his shirtless back and realized he was no longer alone in the room. He had heard no sound of any door or window opening anywhere in the house, which meant his visitor was most likely a demon.

Then, the tendril of sweet perfume reached his nostrils. As flighty and capricious as the Succubus was, her taste in scents hadn't changed much.

"Evening, Caryss," he greeted, without turning to her.

"I've been *Cynthia* for the past four decades now, Raim." Her voice, thick with seduction, wrapped around him before her slender arms circled his waist from behind. "Not that you care." Even without seeing her face, he could tell she was pouting—her plump bottom lip would be slightly extended in a move practiced to perfection.

Her firm, full breasts pressed against his back, her long silky locks tickling his skin.

"You change your human names a few times a century. Remembering them all would be a waste of energy." He turned in her arms to face her.

Caryss's emerald eyes greeted him.

"You remember everything." She waved him off. "You just don't bother talking about any of it."

"You didn't come here to talk about my memories." He picked up a lock of her chestnut hair, absentmindedly twisting it around his finger. "Just as you don't care what name I call you."

The seductive expression slipped off Caryss's face, replaced by that of calm indifference that Raim knew the Succubus only allowed herself to display in his presence.

"True. I don't care about my name, or anyone else's for that matter, as long as they feed me."

"How did you know where to find me?" He freed himself from her embrace and strolled to the armchair by the fireplace.

"I figured you'd be either here or on the island since rumour has it you quit the Council. I checked the castle first, but you weren't there. So, here I am, finding you alone like always, with your music and chocolate." She pointed at the silver tray with pralines by his chair. "Why did you quit?"

She came closer to stand over him.

He considered her question for a moment.

"I believe I'm tired, Caryss." He lifted a dark-chocolate praline off the tray, but waited to eat it, simply holding it in his fingers. "It was exhausting, fighting for the survival of a race that is dead-set on its self-extermination."

She arched a perfectly groomed eyebrow. "Life would have been so much simpler if you went through it completely alone. You'd have no one to worry about but yourself."

"But I am alone. And I don't care for others."

"That's what you say." With a nonchalant little shrug, she knelt in front of him, placing her elbows on his knees. "It is a shame that you and I cannot feed off each other. Some human lives would have been spared if we could."

Raim scanned her, searching past the expensive dress and the luscious body underneath. The unappetizing echoes of emotions of the men Caryss had fed off floated inside her—nothing he could or would take. He was sure she didn't see anything enticing inside him, either.

"It is a shame," he agreed, leaning back in his chair. The praline began to melt in his hand, and he placed it back on the tray, licking the smudge of bittersweet chocolate off his fingers. "Anything new? Or is your visit here simply because you've missed me?"

"Ooh, I always miss you, honey." The pout came out again. Centuries-old habits weren't easily hidden or forgotten. "You will be the only one I'll miss when I leave here, too."

"You're leaving?" The restless nature of the Succubus had taken Caryss around the world a few times during the centuries he had known her. "Where to, this time?"

"Out of here." Rising to her feet, she took a seat in the armchair next to his, facing the fire, too. The high slit of her skirt parted, displaying her long, shapely legs as she crossed them. "I'm leaving this world, Raim. I've come to say goodbye."

"You are?" He laced his fingers in front of him. Something akin to regret tugged at his heart.

Since Caryss had found him, lying on the bottom of a ravine in the Alps, with every bone in his body broken and flesh gnawed off his bones by wolves, she had been the only one he had ever spoken to openly, not as a Grand Master, but as an equal.

"Are you sad about me leaving?" She gazed at him with curiosity.

"Parting from someone you knew for a long time always carries a certain amount of sadness, doesn't it?"

"Not for me." She shook her head. "But that's the difference between us, Raim. You've never been a true demon. No matter how hard you try, you can't escape your angelic nature."

"Angelic?" he scoffed.

He knew Caryss was referring to the place where all Incubi came from. Still, the word seemed ridiculous, for he felt nothing of the Divine in him anymore.

The only thing that remained of that *nature* was the ability to feel the emotions he consumed. That was the reason why during his early centuries on Earth he fed mostly on the aggression of human males he fought in battles. Aggression didn't hurt as some of the other human emotions did, it ignited him from the inside instead.

"Why are you leaving, Caryss?"

She shrugged a delicate shoulder, bare from the green silk of her dress.

"Many of us have left. The times have been changing. Men are more likely to get at home from their wives now what they used to come to me for—"

"Maybe, but that wouldn't mean a shortage of clients for you. There will always be plenty of men in this world willing to feed a Succubus."

Even if feeding one carried a real chance of dying—Caryss wasn't known for her self-control around humans.

The Priory had long abandoned their hope to rein in the Succubi under their control. Even arranging for a meeting with them had proven impossible. Whatever representatives the Priory had sent to hunt, capture or even talk to a Succubus had never returned. The true demons that they were, the Succubi refused to be controlled by any kind of an agreement. The Priory had nothing to force them with and had no choice but to let them be.

It helped that there were too few Succubi in this world to cause devastation on any large scale. Restless and easily bored, they moved between worlds freely, rarely staying in one for longer than a few centuries at a time.

"The taste of human men is turning stale, Raim," Caryss complained. "Their stamina is not what it has been. Besides, some of them end up falling in love, which is simply pathetic. Honestly, sometimes draining them feels like an act of mercy—simply to put them out of their misery."

"I hope you'll find what you're searching for in the next world, Caryss."

"I don't think I will. That must be *my* curse, Raim, to always be looking for something I am not meant to find. Well . . ." She got up in one fluid motion, smoothing the skirt of her dress over her thighs. "Who knows, I might be back in a few centuries to find you here again, listening to Beethoven and eating chocolates." A smile ghosted her lips, subtle enough to be genuine.

"Maybe not." He rose from his chair, too.

For the first time ever, Raim realized he was faced with uncertainty about his future. He sensed there was a change coming. However, he wasn't sure when and what it would be.

"Are you hoping for Forgiveness, too?" She tilted her head, with another flash of curiosity in her green eyes.

"No." That hope had long died, provided he had ever had it in the first place. "The only way for me to end my existence in this world is to be banished to another."

"Would that be something you'd want?"

"It absolutely doesn't matter what I want, Caryss. Here is another difference between us. Unlike you, I cannot move freely between the dimensions. I have been sentenced to this world against my will. Leaving it is also out of my control."

"Well, for what it's worth, I hope *you'll* find what you're searching for, Raim." She came closer, wrapping her arms around his neck. "Goodbye."

He met her lips in a kiss, perfectly executed and void of any true passion on her part, then watched her depart through the wall, the way she must have arrived.

Left alone again, he sank back into his chair. Sadness grew stronger, filling in the void left by her departure. For a while now, Caryss had been the closest to what one would call a 'friend' to him.

'You feel.'

That was a curse on its own. At that moment, Raim envied Caryss's absolute indifference.

'You've lost the bliss of Heaven but never gained the true apathy of Hell,' she told him once. Throughout his life, he often mourned the loss of the former. Right now, he really wished for the numbness of the latter, as the agony of longing intensified, encompassing everything and everyone he had lost over the centuries.

He took a bite of the dark chocolate from the tray and let the morsel melt and coat his tongue with sweetness before swallowing. With the sweet taste slowly vanishing, the bitterness was all that remained.

"Just like a woman," he muttered. "A brief moment of sweetness, followed by an eternity of bitter regrets."

Leaning his head back, he let his mind float with the music filling the room, and unleashed the memories. He could never deny the craving to relive them, bracing for the pain they brought.

Chapter 3

KIEVAN RUS

11th Century

"So, what do you think about this part of the world, Raim?" Gremory brushed in passing the branches of the trees on the riverbank.

The two of them had been walking along the river for two days now.

"Would this place make a good site for the new Incubi Base?"

"Possibly." Raim shrugged. "Just like a few others we have seen so far."

Gremory and he had been sent by the Council to scout farther north from the current Base in the Islamic Empire. With the area there steadily getting too crowded and atmosphere too volatile, the Council had been searching for a new place to move the Base for a few decades now.

After months of traveling, the two of them were ready to return and present their findings.

"There is not much activity around here." Gremory stroked the silvery, furry buds covering the branches of the tree. "No major wars or trading routes, either. Yet a fair number of human settlements, enough to nourish us all. This might work."

"It might," Raim agreed, his brain not really engaging in the conversation. Right now, he was more concerned about the things they needed to do when they reached one of the settlements Gremory was talking about. "We shall get some horses in the next village."

Although Incubi didn't need regular sleep the way humans did, traveling on horseback burned far less energy than walking. It would help them move ahead faster, with fewer stops needed for feeding.

"Steal or buy them?" Gremory glanced his way. Like Raim's, Gremory's eyes were blue. But unlike Raim's pale colour of ice, his partner's were that of the midnight sky, almost indigo. "We have the money, we could just buy the horses."

Raim's skin prickled with both the anticipation and unease he often felt at the prospect of contact with humans. Given the choice, he'd rather move the Base to an area entirely uninhabited by them.

As the Divine would have it, though, the Incubi depended on human energy to keep them awake and alert. Although immortal, when deprived of the energy of humans' emotions for too long, demons would fall into a state of painful torture, innocuously called Deep Sleep.

"I'm starving," Gremory sighed.

It had been days since either of them fed. They both needed some nourishment, which meant getting even closer to humans than Raim felt comfortable with.

"We'll wait until nightfall, then sneak in, feed, and escape before anyone wakes up. We'll make sure to grab some horses on our way out. Stealing them would be simpler."

Their last visit to a human village had not gone all that smoothly. Someone spotted them as they slipped into a house through the locked door, with the intention to enter the dreams of those inside and feed on their emotions. The woman who saw them roused the whole village before they managed to even skim a thing. Raim rolled a shoulder back, still sore from the blow of a broom handle.

Gremory's wound from that encounter was more severe. Raim glanced at his partner's sleeve, dark with dried blood. All because Gremory didn't wring the man's neck, leaving him alive instead, only to be attacked by the very same man again a minute later. The man was wielding a knife that time. The blade had sliced through the back of Gremory's arm, before Raim managed to murder the human.

Conniving, back-stabbing, primitive creatures.

Yet Incubi depended on them as energy sources.

What a cruel joke.

Even worse than the need to feed, was the Incubi's instinct. Inexplicable sympathy towards humans caused most of the demons Raim knew to be lenient when they should be fierce.

Gremory's arm was injured only because he hesitated to kill his attacker on the spot, sparing his life. One had to be ruthless with the vile mortals, Raim had learned.

The reason why the Council sent demons in pairs, Raim believed, was to watch each other's backs. Raim had failed to keep Gremory safe. The faint coppery smell of his partner's blood drifted his way, as if to remind him of that.

"We'll get in at night," he reiterated, firmly. "You'll stay with me at all times. And when you need to kill, promise me you will not hesitate."

Gremory didn't reply right away. Snapping a branch of a tree, he stroked the fuzzy buds, visibly lost in thought.

"Promise," Raim insisted. Gremory had saved Raim from being maimed or mutilated many times. He was the only Incubus Raim trusted without reservation, and he had no doubts he could count on his partner to watch his back. Right now, though, he needed to hear Gremory's promise to put his own safety first, whatever the cost. "We may be immortal but they could still torture us," he gritted through his teeth. "Not to mention that any grave injury would delay our return."

"Let's just be more careful next time," Gremory suggested, promising nothing. "Murder is not always necessary."

The Incubus was obviously in agreement with the strategies of the current Council, which called for demons to stay away from humans as much as possible, instead of gaining an upper hand over them as Raim would have done, if he were in charge.

The next Council election was in the fall, just months away. Hopefully, whoever got to be the Grand Master this time would impose more control and show determination when dealing with humans.

"Fine." Raim snatched the fuzzy tree branch from Gremory's hand and tossed it into the river. "Just keep close to me and stay safe." He marched ahead. "Leave the murder to me."

Chapter 4

THE SHOCK OF THE HEAVY, crudely-made mace smashing into Raim's face shuddered through his entire body. Losing his balance, he crashed to the ground.

"*Nechisty*!" His assailant spat the word at him, hurriedly following his first blow with another before Raim had a chance to get up.

Nechisty—Dirty, impure.

The word referred to an evil spirit.

Raim and Gremory had managed to feed by skimming in the village that night. However, they had been spotted walking through a barn wall while trying to steal the horses.

Now, they had been pursued and attacked as both thieves *and* evil spirits.

Raim rolled on the ground, crushing the new spring grass, in an attempt to escape another blow from the mace fitted with iron spikes, but the blow never came. Through the red fog clouding his vision, Raim saw the tip of Gremory's sword emerge through the chest of the human who brandished the mace.

Relief and gratitude spread warm inside him as the human collapsed into the first-in-the-year blue flowers, next to Raim.

Unlike the Incubus, the man was dead.

At least four more pounced on Gremory, though, wielding whatever weapons they got their hands on, from maces, to axes, to pitchforks. Loud shouting from across the field announced the arrival of reinforcements from the village.

Too many for Gremory to deal with on his own, Raim realized with dread.

Rolling to his belly, he propped his hands and knees into the ground, trying to heave himself up to come to his partner's aid.

His consciousness floated into a red, throbbing fog. His arms shook, giving in shortly and sending him rolling to the ground again. The sound of clashing weapons grew distant.

Then the world went dark.

IT COULDN'T HAVE BEEN much later when Raim's vision returned, although the sky was already bright and blue, the sun having fully risen over the horizon. He and Gremory had been attacked right before dawn, and it was full morning now.

The thought of the fight jolted him with alarm. If the humans found him in this state, it wouldn't take them long to incapacitate him again, possibly for a very long and painful time. There was no way of knowing what they'd do while he was unconscious. He had been buried alive before, and he had heard accounts from others about being burnt, decapitated, and dismembered.

No matter what was done to their physical bodies, Incubi always healed completely, returning to their original form. No scars, no missing limbs, no deformities. The process of healing, however, took time and was no less painful than that of humans.

Gathering his arms and legs under him, Raim struggled to his feet. The bones in his limbs had not been broken, he noted with relief. It meant he could walk away from here and hide.

Picking up his sword off the ground, he stumbled towards the tree line of the forest in the distance. He had to find a safe spot to hide and wait to see if Gremory came back in search of him.

WAITING IN THE FOREST for the rest of the day, Raim caught no sign of either the villagers or Gremory.

His head throbbed with agonizing pain. The injuries he sustained had swollen as the healing process began. While he couldn't visually inspect the wound to his head, when he tried to touch his face, his hand encountered a mangled mess of crushed bone, tissue, and blood.

He must have lost his left eye, for whatever vision he had only came from the right one, now. Although, that one had been slowly swelling shut, too.

Healing took energy he didn't have. He needed to feed.

Ironically, feeding meant searching out the humans he wished to avoid. Stumbling to his feet, he headed south, deciding against returning to the village where the attackers had come from.

He trudged in that direction for a while. At nightfall, the faint smell of chimney smoke finally reached his nostrils—another human settlement, a food source for him. Following the smell of the smoke, he reached the first log house on the outskirts of the village sometime close to midnight.

Angry since the human attack last night, hurting from his wounds, and starving, Raim didn't pause at the tall wooden fence, brazenly walking right through it. At the sight of him, the dog, chained in the yard, whimpered and retreated under the stairs, tail tucked between its legs.

Without breaking his stride, Raim walked through the logs of the house wall and into the large, dark kitchen, which appeared to also serve as the bedroom and the common room.

The fire in the stove had gone out, with only a few embers still glowing orange. Loud snoring brought his attention to the low bed covered with furs next to the stove, where it was the warmest. A couple slept under the covers. The man lay on his back, snoring like a family of wild boars. The woman turned in what must have been a fitful sleep, tossing aside the bear hide they used for a cover.

Pressing his back to the wall, Raim slid to her side of the bed, then sat down on the floor and hurriedly entered her dreams, uninvited.

The warm smell of cattle and fresh hay immediately wrapped around his mind. In the semi-darkness, he spotted the woman's white linen nightshirt as she lay in the pile of hay in the barn of her dream.

It was pretty here. Raim noticed some bright fresh flowers that wouldn't be found in hay in real life. A few tendrils of milky-white fog floated through the air, filling it with a freshness the woman's small house lacked in reality.

She seemed content, even if a bit restless, as she rolled to her back, bending her legs at the knees. Her long shirt slid up to her hips.

Her eyes were closed, but Raim knew that *here* she wasn't sleeping. Quietly, he snuck closer, willing her not to open her eyes, lest she see his disfigured face and have her dream turn into a nightmare.

Kneeling into the hay at her side, he slid the tips of his fingers up the inside of her arm gently, like a caress that could be easily mistaken for the tickle of grass.

Her chest rose with an inhale, pleasure coming in a swell that Raim quickly skimmed. Gliding his hand down her arm, he touched the inside of her thigh next, watching her skin ripple with goosebumps as a wave of delicious arousal reached him with her moan.

Her response encouraged him to go further, his hunger urging him to do more.

Propping himself on his elbow at her side, he ran his fingers up her body and cupped her breast through the linen shirt. Pushing against the rough fabric, her nipple was already pebble-hard when he brushed his thumb over it.

Muttering something under her breath, she rolled closer to him, hooking her leg over his hip.

Her desire flushed him like a tidal wave, soothing his pain and filling him with the energy he so badly needed.

"I want your cock in me, Milan," the woman murmured, thrusting her hips into him.

Raim shifted away a little. Whoever *Milan* was, Raim had no intention of filling in for the man. All he wanted was to feed, to ease his pain and hunger.

He tentatively slid his hand between his body and hers. She squirmed impatiently, reaching for him as if for a kiss.

Her eyes opened.

Her blissful expression melted away quickly, replaced by a grimace of horror—at seeing his mangled face, no doubt.

She screamed.

The sound, like a blow to his chest, kicked him out of her dream. Finding himself back on the floor, it took Raim a moment to orientate himself in reality.

The woman's screams had followed him here, slicing through his aching head like a knife blade.

"What by *chyort* is going on?" A gruff male voice cursed. The husband's snoring had stopped abruptly. He was now sitting on the bed, rubbing the sleep out of his eyes.

"Vazlav, look! He is here!" The woman shrieked, scurrying off the bed. "The *chyort!*—Demon!" She frantically gestured at Raim as he rose to his feet.

Clearly, it was time for him to leave. Without sparing a glance at either of them, Raim headed for the wall through which he had come.

There was no fear in him, not even a concern about the possibility of another attack. The rage left from the last one doused it all, and he hurried to get out before the hurt and anger boiling inside him could explode, claiming the innocents.

"Argh!"

The sound made him pivot back the same moment as the woman's husband, Vazlav, hacked an axe into Raim's shoulder. *"Sgin, nechisty!*—Disappear, evil!"

Wincing from the pain that shot down from his shoulder through his chest, Raim grabbed the man by his throat.

The faint spice of aggression filtered from the human to him. It blended with the fury inside Raim, setting it off. As if the man sensed it, the rotten stench of fear emanated from him in foul waves.

Clenching his teeth, Raim reached deeper, searching for the clear light of Vazlav's life force. Finding it, he took it all in one gulp.

"Look what you've done," he said calmly to the wailing woman, even as a storm raged inside him, threatening to consume him. "You got your man killed." He dropped the lifeless body to the floor.

"Vaslav!" With an ear-splitting scream, the woman scurried to her dead husband.

"Maybe Milan's cock would be of some consolation," Raim threw over his shoulder on his way out, clenching his trembling hands into fists, "now that you are a widow."

Chapter 5

RAIM STOMPED BACK TO the woods.

The swelling of his injured face had all but closed his one good eye by now, leaving him to find his way in the dark mostly by touch and instincts. His head throbbed violently, almost making him wish his attacker had cut it off completely. And the fresh wound on his shoulder ached, making it difficult to lift his arm, not to mention to use his sword.

The long journey back to the Base wouldn't be easy in this state. With him rapidly running out of whatever morsels of energy he had managed to skim from the woman in her sleep chances were, he'd collapse in a few days if he didn't find more nourishment soon.

It would be wise to search for a safe place to hide and heal. Only, he needed to have humans nearby for feeding. Otherwise, falling into Deep Sleep in the middle of nowhere carried a risk of staying in that state for an unknown amount of time.

Afraid of not being able to get up if he stopped, Raim kept walking.

Soon the night ended, replaced by a pale early-spring morning that eventually rolled into another day. The pain continued to wrack Raim's body. Everything hurt with the same intensity. He was no longer able to tell which agony came from the injuries and which was the pain of hunger.

Even in the daylight, he could hardly see anything around him. His right eye had swollen shut, and it took him a painful effort to open it enough to be able to peek through a narrow slit.

Late in the afternoon, the trees had parted, leading him into a clearing with a narrow creek in the middle.

Raim knelt by the water, cupping some with his hands. He never felt thirsty, but the sensation of the cool water rushing down his throat as he drank it was refreshing. The weight of it settling in his stomach fooled his hunger for a few moments, too.

Rinsing his hands, he splashed some water on his face, careful not to touch his injuries so as not to aggravate the pain. The agony of hunger, though, was now the one that tortured him the most.

With a groan, he leaned back into the grass on the bank of the creek, letting his swollen eyelids shut completely. The warmth of sunshine seeped pleasantly through his armour and tunic.

'Just for a few minutes,' he told himself, though he knew that taking a break was dangerous. Every second that passed drained more energy out of his body.

He felt worn and exhausted. The unpleasant feeling at the memory of his last feeding scratched inside him with guilt that he did not want to acknowledge. Killing the man did not sit well with him, though admitting it appeared to be a weakness at this point.

It was because of humans that he was in pain right now, separated from Gremory and disfigured. He should hate and despise them, not let the guilt gnaw at him.

Anger flickered inside him, and he let it build, feeding it with more hatred.

Humans were weak creatures. Aggression and reckless courage often were the only positive emotions in many he had encountered.

Why should *he* feel any guilt when they kept murdering each other constantly? Most had even less reasons for killing than he had. And few suffered from any guilt at all.

Raim shouldn't be the one running away and hiding from them. Incubi were stronger and immortal. When organized properly, the few hundred of them could bring into submission thousands of humans.

He wanted to see demons come out of hiding.

Humans, weak and pathetic as they were, needed to be contained at the Base as food sources. Having nourishment available at all times would be a sure way to end the hunger that had tortured demons from the moment they first appeared in this world.

If the Council members were too blind or too weak to realize the Incubi's true purpose in this world—domination—then Raim would have to force them to see that.

Plans churned in his head, giving birth to ambition. With only months left until the next election, there was still enough time to contest the position of Grand Master for himself.

Lost in his thoughts, he didn't hear the footsteps or the rustle of the reeds from someone approaching. A slight tug at the sword in his hand snapped him back to reality. Somebody was obviously trying to pry his prized weapon out of his hold.

Jolted into a sitting position, he couldn't open his eyes. Fresh blood had seeped from the wound on his face, caking solid over his one good eye while he had lain there in the sun. He blindly raised the sword in front of him.

"Who is here?"

"You're alive?" a female voice exclaimed with a gasp.

"Stay back!" he shouted, menacingly thrusting the sword in the direction of the voice. "Who are you and how many of you are here?"

"You can't see, can you?" she replied, a little calmer this time. "There are, um . . . a dozen of us here." Her tone betrayed her. He knew she was lying, even before she added, "All big, strong men. Except for me, of course."

The statement confirmed she was bluffing. Men would not have let a woman speak on their behalf. That, combined with the lack of noise if a large group of men indeed surrounded him, assured Raim that he was one on one with the woman.

A food source.

The thought flashed through his brain, giving him hope.

"Could you help me get up?" he asked, schooling his voice into a friendlier tone. "Please?" He stretched his bare hand her way. All he needed was one touch—skin-to-skin.

"How are you still alive with your head smashed in like that?" Distrust and suspicion were in her voice, with no sound of her coming closer. "I thought you were an *utoplennik*—a corpse of a drowned man—washed up on the side of the creek."

"So, you came here to loot my weapons?" Resentment slipped into his tone, no matter how hard he tried to hold it back.

Vile creatures.

Male and female.

"Your armour and your clothes, too," the woman admitted. "Those are some fine things you have there. Why would I let them rot?"

Raim drew in a deep breath, collecting his thoughts. Blind as he was, he couldn't even skim any emotions off her unless she touched him. To get her to come closer, he needed her to let down her guard.

"If you help me to get up, I may consider gifting you some of what I have." He instilled as much sweetness as he could into his voice. "Even my sword."

There was no way he would ever part with his weapon, but the woman didn't know that.

"What good is a sword," she retorted, "if I have no one to wield it to protect me should you choose to hurt me—"

She must have caught her own mistake, as she cut herself short.

"What about that dozen strong men you have with you?" he couldn't help teasing.

She huffed quietly, probably taking a moment to gather her wits.

"You know what?" she snapped. "I don't need anyone to take care of myself. And I don't need your stupid sword."

The rustle of grass alerted him of her departure, sending him up to his feet in alarm. Who knew how long it would take him, practically blind and starving, to stumble upon another Source? He needed to keep this one, at all cost.

"Wait!" He rubbed his eye vigorously, desperate for it to open. If he could see her emotions, he could skim them or at least figure out more accurately what to say to soothe her hostility and mistrust. "I'm not going to harm you, promise."

"Oh, I know you won't." A mocking note rang through her voice. "Because I'm not coming close enough for you to do that."

The damn eyelid finally obeyed, Raim had rubbed enough of the dried blood away to open his one good eye. Squinting in the bright sunlight, he saw the dark-haired woman in the middle of the creek. Holding her long brown skirt up, she hopped from rock to rock, crossing to the other side.

"Wait! I swear I'm not going to harm you." He rushed to the creek after her. "I am a good, decent man," he lied.

"A *good* man is a dead man," she threw over her shoulder, climbing up the opposite bank. "Since you've turned out to be alive, I want nothing to do with you."

"I'll pay you!" he shouted at her back in desperation, then noted with hope that she slowed her steps a bit. "In gold. How much do you want?" He shook the leather pouch at his waist, making the heavy coins inside clink.

These were the dinars from the Islamic Empire that he had received from the Council for this journey. The money was for travel expenses, like buying a horse instead of stealing one, or fixing his armour if it got damaged in a scuffle.

They were a long way from the Empire here, deep into Kievan Rus, but gold was appreciated by humans everywhere. Wasn't it? The woman proved it by stopping and glancing back over her shoulder.

"How do I know you're not lying?"

"Here!" He tossed her the coin he had fished out of his purse.

She promptly caught it in the air, inspected it quickly and bit at it, then examined it even more closely.

"I haven't seen one like this before. Where is it from?"

"South." He gestured in that general direction.

"Are you a Pecheneg?" she asked, fear hardening her guarded expression, though a tiny tendril of curiosity filtered through it as well. Unfortunately, she remained too far for Raim to skim that. "Grandmother told me about them coming from the South or South-East all the way to Kiev a long time ago. They burned villages, killed many people, and took even more as slaves. I've heard they have black hair, like mine, and skin darker than that of my people. Like yours."

"I'm not a Pecheneg," he assured her. "I came from the Islamic Empire. People there have dark hair, like yours, too." His own colouring had nothing to do with any geographic location—he was a demon, not a human. But she didn't need to know about that. Slowly, he ventured a small step in her direction, reducing the distance between them, although still too far for him to skim anything useful.

Not that she felt many positive emotions at the moment, anyway. Most of what he saw inside her was hostility and suspicion, with some interest for the coins in his purse and curiosity about his person.

"Do they also have dark skin like yours?" She slid her gaze along his arm to his bare hand. "I've never seen anyone like you before."

"Some have even darker if you cross the sea to Africa." He nodded, stepping closer as she continued to stare at his hand with clear fascination on her face. That sense of wonder floating inside her was what he was after, inching closer in an attempt to skim it.

"Darker than yours?" Her eyes flew open wider as she muttered, "The world beyond these woods is full of wonder. Does the sun where you come from burn stronger? Were you born like that, or did your colour change as you grew up?"

He wasn't *born*. Telling her that would most definitely spook her into fleeing. Feeling too exhausted to come up with another lie at the moment, he settled for something in the middle, "I've always had this skin colour, for as long as I've been in this world."

She fingered the long braid draped over her shoulder. "I was born with black hair," she said. "People say I have a black eye, too—"

"Just one?" he attempted a joke, hoping to lift her suspicion against him.

She didn't laugh.

"My eyes are dark brown. But that's a saying. 'Having a black eye' means to have the power to do bad things to others. And maybe I do have that power." She narrowed her eyes at him, menacingly.

"Do you wish me ill?" he asked, suddenly feeling curious himself.

"*Ill?*" she snorted a laugh. "Look at yourself, stranger! You already are as ill as they come. Your wound will fester soon if it hasn't already. I'd wager you'll be dead before the new moon—no need for me to harm you any further."

"Could you help me, then?" He realized he was grasping at straws in his attempts to manipulate her emotions. The cautious mistrust seemed deeply rooted inside this girl. "Could you use your *powers* to help me heal, woman? In exchange for a payment, of course."

She took a moment to reply. "How many gold coins do you have?"

"How many would you want for your trouble?"

She wrinkled her forehead, giving him a sideways glance. "Five."

"I'll give you three." A rush of renewed hope coursed through him. "You can keep that one." He tipped his chin at her fist clutching his gold. "I'll give you two more when I'm feeling well enough to continue on my journey."

"What exactly do you expect from me? Just a place to stay?"

Fear leaped high inside her.

"I'll stay anywhere you would deem appropriate," he rushed to reassure her.

Hopefully, she would lower her guard enough to feel something more agreeable to his taste than guarded wariness.

Either way, Raim was fully intending to take off as soon as he felt better. He had big things to accomplish, and this woman here was just another meal for him on the way there.

"How about you stay right where you are?" she replied, with challenge. "I find *that* the most appropriate place for you."

Her words did not fool him, though. The hook of promised money, aided by genuine curiosity, was already clearly deep inside her. All he had left to do was to reel her in, carefully.

"Alright, but what am I paying you for, then? If you're leaving me here now, I want my money back."

He stretched his hand out her way, and she quickly hid her fist with his gold behind her back. The desire for the coin clearly warred with caution in her. The enticing wisp of curiosity was swirling among those two emotions.

Keeping his swollen eyelid open was growing more difficult. He let his eye close, switching tactics.

"I am not a threat, woman. I will not harm you." Raim sat down on the bank of the creek and dropped his head into his hands, elbows propped on his knees. "You said it yourself. I'll be dead soon. You can leave me here to die, or do the right thing and find me a quiet place to rest in peace."

The pause that followed filled him with trepidation as he waited for her answer, hoping that sitting slouched, he appeared less threatening to her and more in need of help.

"Are you alone?" she asked finally. "Or are there more of you nearby?"

"I am completely on my own. There is no one else, anywhere near." That could possibly be true. Gremory could be well on his way to the Base by now, for all Raim knew.

"Throw me your sword," she demanded.

Opening his eye proved to be impossible, this time. Blindly, Raim took off the scabbard with his sword and tossed it in the direction of her voice. He would make sure to get his weapon back from her later, after she had *fed* him back to health.

By the rustling of the reeds, he figured she made her way to where the sword had landed and picked it up. Next came the sound of her drawing it out of its sheath.

"Cross to this side now," she ordered. "But keep your distance."

Feeling his way to the creek, he stumbled into the cool water, his boots taking it in and chilling his feet.

"It's not deep here. Barely knee-high," she assured him. "Don't come any closer," she warned as he scrambled up the bank to her.

"I can't see." Raim stretched his arms in front of him. Keeping his distance as ordered wasn't easy since he had no way of knowing exactly how far she was from him.

"You can't? That's actually a good thing," she replied gruffly. He then felt something hard under his fingers and realized it was the end of his scabbard. "Hold on to this and follow me," she directed then warned, "If you try to come any closer than that, I'll kill you with your own sword."

"Deal." He followed her lead through the grassy clearing. "What's your name?"

"Olyena," she replied after a moment of hesitation.

She did not ask him for his name in return.

Chapter 6

"CLOSE IT, QUICKLY." Reaching around Raim, Olyena slammed the door shut as soon as they crossed the threshold he had nearly tripped over in his blindness. "Don't let the chickens out."

"What chickens?" he asked, dumbfounded.

Her chest brushed by his arm, and he grasped at the air around him in search of her hand, but she moved away before he could catch it.

"*My* chickens." She was moving around the place she had brought him to, busy with some activity he couldn't see. "I've already lost two over the winter. A fox got one. Not sure what happened to the other one. Might have been a wolf or a fox, too."

Raim stood where she had left him. The air inside indeed smelled like a chicken coup, with the fairly pleasant aroma of cooked human food mixed in.

He heard the loud clanking of metal on wood—Olyena must have dropped the sword on a bench or a table. The thought of her putting down the weapon brought some relief. Being stabbed by the woman, one guarded and on edge, would not have improved his situation.

"Come." She shoved at his back unexpectedly, urging him to move forward. "Sit down and let me take a look." Pressing on his shoulders, she made him plop onto a surface covered by some bedding—possibly a cot or a bed.

"Where are we? Anywhere near a village?" he asked with some hope. As evasive as this woman had proven to be, Raim didn't discount the possibility of feeding off someone else.

There was no noise that usually came with a human settlement of any size, though. The time it took them to reach here also hadn't been that long. Raim doubted they had even left the forest.

"No village," she replied curtly, rattling with what sounded like dishes. Then he heard the clear noise of water being poured into one. "I live here . . ." she set the dish on a hard surface next to where he was sitting, and moved closer. "Alone. The nearest village is a day away. There is no one here to help you but me." She instilled a certain gravity into her words, undoubtedly wanting Raim to know that it was in his best interest not to hurt her.

"I promised I would not harm you."

"So you did," she muttered, still with more suspicion than trust in her voice.

He heard the noise of water again, then felt a warm, wet cloth tentatively touch his face. No matter how slight the contact was, the pain still made him wince.

"No one has cleaned it." Olyena gently moved the cloth around his wound. "Grandmother always told me that dirt made it worse."

"Where is your grandmother?"

"Dead." Her reply was clipped. "This is a grave injury you have here . . ."

"How about the rest of your family?" he found himself asking. "Your mother? Father—" he cut himself short, suddenly distracted by another touch.

Skin-to-skin contact.

The thumb of her hand holding the cloth brushed by his chin as she continued to clean the wound on his face, and he forgot all he was about to say.

Her positive emotions remained shrouded in fear and mistrust. Yet a clear streak of compassion reached him from inside of that dark cloud. Pure, nourishing, and fresh. Hitting all his senses at once, it filled him whole, momentarily muting the pain and even the hunger.

Unable to hold back a groan of satisfaction, he leaned away from her, lest he take more and scare her.

"Did I hurt you?" She sounded concerned, and he wished she had kept touching him so he could skim her concern for him, too. "Your face feels cold," she muttered. "As if you were already dead."

The note of fear in her voice snapped Raim back to attention. Taking her emotion through skin-to-skin contact created a cooling sensation in her hand, making him seem cold like a corpse to her.

The last thing he needed was for Olyena to convince herself that he was the undead, walking the earth—or something of similar nature. Human imagination had no boundaries and often needed just a spark to burst into panic.

"Of course I'm not dead." He smiled, keeping his voice light. "Just *deadly* tired. Here." He stretched his hand her way, palm up. "Touch it again if you will. I'm not well, but not dead yet."

It took a long moment before he heard the soft rustling of her clothes as she leaned his way, then felt the light, tentative stroke of her fingers along his palm. Calling on all self-control he could master, Raim resisted taking the slightest tendril of her emotions this time. None, whatsoever.

He needed a lot of energy to get well in a timely manner, but to get more from her, he realized he had to earn her trust first.

"Hmm." She patted his hand, a little more firmly as her caution eased somewhat. "You *are* warm. Not excessively though, which is good. It means you're not running a fever."

He sat completely still under her touch, afraid even to draw a breath. It must have given her more confidence, as she placed his hand between both of hers.

"This is strange," she muttered under her breath. "I gather it has been at least a day since you were hurt. Yet a fever has yet to set in." She touched the skin around the injury on his face. "This must have been quite a blow . . . What did it?"

The fingers of her one hand remained wrapped around his. Through that contact, Raim *saw* clearly the sharp flash of compassion in her. Even heavily blended with pity as it was, it would still be nourishing enough for him. He could already taste it in his mind—the heady rush of reviving energy it would bring.

Extremely carefully, he allowed himself to skim some of it, making sure not to *take* any, to avoid causing another chilly sensation in her hand. He then tore his mind away from the visual of her emotions and forced himself to focus on her words instead.

"Mace," he replied to her question. "It was the blow of a mace."

"That would do it." She released a long exhale. "Your nose is destroyed. The cheekbone has been broken. The left eye is gone," she listed his losses calmly, with a detachment of a healer assessing the work ahead of her. "I can't believe you're still alive. Spirits must really want you to live. I'll see if I can help, but even if you survive, you'll remain disfigured."

"I don't care about that."

"True." He sensed her shrug. "What good is beauty to a man, anyway. Even to a woman it often brings nothing but trouble."

Letting go of his hand, Olyena moved away, and he exhaled the tension out of his chest.

"I'll make you some rowanberry tea in a minute. I also cooked some dried mushroom soup this morning. It's still warm. That's all I have."

"I'm not hungry."

"You're not? I wonder how that feels. I don't remember the last time I was really full." She shuffled some pots on the stove, by the sound of it. "You need to eat to get better. I don't have much food left after the winter, but I get a few eggs from the chickens every now and then. First thing tomorrow morning, I'll check the traps I have set, too. We may get a squirrel or even a rabbit if we're lucky."

Listening to her chatter, Raim let his body relax in the warmth of this place. Even the throbbing in his head had quieted down somewhat.

He'd stay here for a few days, he decided. The morsels of Olyena's positive emotions should sustain him for a little while, at least until his injuries had healed to the point that his vision returned and the physical pain receded.

Taking off his boots, he stretched out on the bed, welcoming the chance to rest at last.

Chapter 7

RAIM KICKED HIS FOOT, tossing the damn chicken off his leg. Judging by the pinkish haze behind his closed eyelid, it must be morning already. Whatever ointment Olyena put on his face last night had crusted hard overnight, making his skin itch. He felt that scratching at it would make it worse, though.

The past two days had been spent mostly lying in bed in Olyena's home. By now, he knew this was indeed where she lived, alone save for the company of two annoying chickens. Unable to do much more than to lie in bed, Raim had been doing just that, diverting every smidgen of energy he managed to steal from Olyena into the healing of his physical body.

His eyes were still not functioning for him to visually inspect his surroundings, and he had been relying on his other senses to orientate himself.

A chicken jumped on his leg again, and he shoved it away.

"Hey!" he heard Olyena's voice, still a bit gruff from sleep. "Be nice to Ryaba. She got us breakfast this morning."

"The chicken?"

"Who else?" The noise of the woman moving through the small space reached him as she bustled about starting a fire and getting ready for the day. "Just about time, too. I haven't had a thing from her for weeks. I'd started to think we should have chicken soup for dinner one day soon."

"You still have the gold I gave you," he reminded, sitting up and leaning with his back against the wall. His body protested with pain, but it was a dull ache now, one he could bare much easier. "Why wouldn't you trade that for food? You said there was a village a day's walk from here?"

She took her time to answer, energetically rattling with the dishes somewhere by the stove.

"So?" he insisted, wondering about the reason for her silence. "Is there a village?"

"Yes." A hard note in her tone gave him notice. "*Less* than a day's walk, actually."

"There you go. All your food problems can be solved within hours."

She didn't reply, silently getting breakfast ready.

"You don't want to go?" Raim asked, wishing more than ever that he could *see* what she was feeling.

This was by far the longest time he had ever spent in the company of a human. Having nothing but her voice to decipher her emotions by was proving extremely difficult.

"I will go," she said softly. "Maybe. Once you get better."

"Why wait?"

"Well, for one, I can't leave you here all alone, can I?" she replied, somewhat abruptly. "You're blind as a bat."

Despite her tone, something new and warm flickered inside Raim's chest. He knew he could count on Gremory to fight in his defence. However, no one had ever taken care of him before Olyena.

"I am sufficiently functional on my own," he assured her. "Even blind."

"All right." There wasn't much conviction in her voice.

He heard the noise of a bowl being placed on the stool next to him. Then, the now familiar, warm scent of her reached him as she sat on the edge of the bed.

Something flipped inside his stomach at her nearness—the feeling too unsettling to be enjoyable, yet too exciting to be unwelcome.

"Let me see how it is today," she said softly, washing off the layer of whatever muddy goo she called 'ointment' that she had smeared all over his face last night. The stuff had dried into a hard crust since then. She soaked it with warm water, gently wiping it off as it turned softer.

The same putrid odour filled the air as it had when she first applied it.

"This thing is vile," Raim complained, wondering once again why he allowed her to subject him to whatever 'treatments' she kept inventing.

Because fussing over him, oddly, created positive emotions in her, he reminded himself. It also brought her physically close enough for him to skim them.

"I've added a few things to my grandmother's recipe," she chatted, cleaning his face. "And I think I am onto something here. The swelling is all but gone now."

Raim had no heart to tell her that being a demon, he would eventually heal no matter what. Had she rolled him in honey and chicken feathers or left him to soak in a mud puddle, all his injuries would eventually heal, one way or another—wholly and completely—regardless of her efforts or despite them.

Hearing how happy she sounded at the progress, though, he kept quiet.

"Would you look at this?" she exclaimed triumphantly.

"I would love to *look*," he replied, more gruffly than he felt. "But I cannot, remember?"

"Just give me a minute." She cleaned the remainder of the stinky stuff off his face, then rinsed the cloth and wiped around his right eye gently. "Can you try to open it, now?"

The healing skin itched, and he lifted his hand to his face to scratch at it.

"Don't rub it," she warned, quickly grabbing his hand. And he *saw* all her emotions at once, holding back from taking any.

She felt at ease around him right now, proud of the job she thought she'd done, hopeful . . . for him.

Slowly, he pried his eye open, looking forward to seeing her face again, much closer this time.

Her dark, expectant gaze greeted him. "And?" she asked, eagerly. "How does it feel?"

"I can see again." He stared at the swirls of tantalizing emotions that curled around her lovely face. "Thank you, Olyena." He skimmed them all, greedily, then immediately closed his eye again, lest she notice the blue light of their reflection in it.

Only then did he realize that this was the first time since he met her that he called her by her name.

"How are you feeling?" she repeated.

The worry in her tone prompted Raim to open his eye. He quite liked the sight of the light, colourful cloud framing her youthful face. The idea of anything marring it displeased him.

"Better. I'm definitely on the mend. Thanks to your skill and expertise." The lie was definitely worth the effort. Her pale cheeks flushed the prettiest shade of pink, a warm tendril of orange brightening the kaleidoscope of her emotions.

"The forest spirits must be on your side. I've never seen anyone recover from wounds like yours before." Shifting closer, she gently slid the tunic off his shoulder and started changing the dressing on his wound there, too.

As needless as Olyena's ministrations were, Raim didn't mind her fussing, enduring even the revolting smell of her potions. Watching her from under his lashes, he continued skimming every single positive emotion felt by her. Aware of the occasional light brush of her fingers over the bare skin of his chest or shoulder, he resisted taking any outright, not wanting to scare her with the chilling sensation again.

"Is the pain better yet?" she asked, not lifting her gaze to his.

"It is." He wasn't really paying much attention to the physical pain at the moment, busy filling himself with her emotions.

"Good. I'll dress your shoulder again but will leave your face uncovered. Sometimes healing is better in the fresh air," she talked animatedly as her hands continued their work. "Now that you can see again, I feel better about you being alone for a bit. I'll leave you some soup for lunch and will go check some of my traps deeper in the woods today."

Having finished her work on his wounds, she got up. He watched her move around the tight dark place inside what appeared to be a log cabin with a dirt floor. Two brown chickens scratched, near the stone stove in the corner.

Olyena brought over a clay plate and placed it on the stool by his side.

"I'm not hungry." He shook his head at the sight of a fried egg.

"You keep saying that." She shoved a crudely made wooden spoon into his hand. "I told you that to keep getting better you need to eat. Are you worried I won't be able to provide for both of us?" She narrowed her eyes at him.

He resisted gliding his gaze down her figure under her stare, but even without a close examination, it was obvious that Olyena hadn't eaten her fill for some time now. The long, wide skirt and the thick shawl she had tied over her shirt across her chest couldn't hide how painfully thin she was.

"No, I am confident in your abilities," he replied mechanically, unable to shake the unpleasant feeling growing inside him.

"Well, then, you eat when I tell you to eat." She shoved the plate closer to him. "And leave it up to me to find the food. You paid me to take care of you, remember?"

He was paying her for a quiet place to heal and a chance to have her close enough to feed off her emotions while he was healing. As for the rest, Olyena somehow had taken it all upon herself on her own. Dressing his wounds and feeding him food was unnecessary for him, but obviously meant something to her.

The discovery that she had been sharing the food she could hardly spare, gave him a sour taste in his mouth. His insides suddenly felt as if filled with acid.

"Do you want me to come with you?" He tried to sound casual, not even looking at the fried egg. "To check on the traps?"

"Why? No, you need to rest." She gestured at the bed. "I won't be long."

"Well, you have this then." He thrust the plate with the egg her way. "If I'm staying in bed all day, I don't need the energy this would provide."

"You have to get better," she protested stubbornly, even as her gaze flickered to the egg.

"I . . ." he drew in a lungful of air, making the sudden decision to come clean, right then and there. "I really don't need to eat, Olyena."

"What do you mean?" She cocked her head. "All men eat."

"*Men* do, but not me."

Silence hung in the room, following his words.

After a moment, her eyes opened wider. Curiosity, surprise, and a hint of the old mistrust filled her. But the sense of wonder that he had recognized in her before, eventually prevailed.

"Are the forest spirits really protecting you?" she asked finally. "Is that why you're healing so well? Is it because you're one of them?"

"Something like that." It was best to let her believe in whatever made more sense to her.

"Is that truly so?" Sitting on the bed next to him, she stared at him openly. "You are a forest spirit? I've never met one of you before. My grandmother did, she told me herself. She saw a forest spirit in the woods one night." Her gaze roaming along his face and body, Olyena lifted her hand to touch the edge of his jaw, then to stroke a strand of his hair that had fallen over his shoulder. "You look so . . . human, though. Grandmother spoke of hair like a mane of grass and leaves, skin coarse like a tree bark, arms long and knotted like oak branches . . ." She traced her fingers down his sleeve, wrapping her hand over his. "Your skin colour may be somewhat similar to that of a young oak's bark, but these are a man's hands."

He kept his eye open, staring straight at her, as he feasted on her wonder and excitement. This time, he allowed her to see the light of their reflection as he skimmed them. With a soft cry, she leaned away from him.

"Your eye . . ." A dark flare of fear flashed inside her at the sight of the blue light in his eye.

"Not that human after all, is it?" He gave her a reassuring smile, not enjoying seeing Olyena afraid.

Thankfully, any trace of mistrust or fear in her disappeared quickly, replaced by hope.

"Did you come here to protect me?"

"Why aren't you afraid of me?" he wondered out loud, puzzled by the reactions of this woman. She feared him when she thought him a man, yet seemed much more comfortable now that she had learned he was not.

"Should I be afraid?" She tilted her head. "Are you an *evil* spirit?"

"Most people don't take the time to figure any of that out before attacking me in terror."

"Most people," she echoed, "are worse than any evil spirit could be."

Chapter 8

OLYENA WENT TO CHECK her traps later that morning. Before she left, Raim insisted she tell him what chores needed to be done around the house. She mentioned an old oak tree that fell near her cabin over winter and said she was planning to chop some of it for wood.

After she was gone, he searched around her small, dark cabin, managing to locate an old axe. Shoo-ing at the chickens to make them stay at the back wall, he opened the front door and left the cramped space.

From the outside, the cabin appeared even smaller. Dark logs, with dried moss stuffed in between, were carved with symbols and letters in a language even he didn't recognize. Strings with dried frogs and chicken feet hung from the rafters and the wooden shutters on the small window. On the gable above the door, Raim saw the head of a black goat, complete with horns and a long beard.

Made of dark, weathered logs and with those odd decorations, the cabin had an eerie, unwelcoming appearance—quite different from its cramped but cozy interior.

'Maybe I do have that power.' He recalled Olyena's words from the day they first met.

The power to do bad things to others.

Raim had seen inside her. He had tasted her emotions. Nothing in this woman spoke of any energy from another world. He was confident she was just a regular human, like the rest of them.

Circling around the cabin, he examined its spooky décor. The dried bat wings, some odd stick figures dangling off strings, the goat head over the entrance—all had the obvious purpose to warn and intimidate.

He recalled the hostility he had glimpsed in Olyena when she spoke of humans, back when she thought him to be one, too. Instead of fighting the accusations of having the *power of the black eye*, she seemed to have embraced it, using it as her defence, as means to enforce her isolation from others.

Curiosity kept his thoughts on his hostess as he tramped through the undergrowth in search of the fallen oak she had mentioned.

He found it a few hundred paces away from the cabin. The trunk was rotten and hollowed from the inside, but thick. It would have taken at least two men to wrap their arms around it when it was a living tree.

Ripping his tunic off over his head, Raim tossed it aside and got to work.

"HOW IS YOUR SHOULDER?" Raim heard Olyena's voice behind his back.

"Fine." He straightened, turning around.

The sun had moved well towards the west by now. Despite the flimsy axe that threatened to snap in his grip, he had managed to cut a couple of short round logs from the trunk and had chopped them into smaller pieces that would fit into Olyena's stove.

"What is that?" She pointed at the amulet around his neck. The teardrop *soros* stone glowed softly in the afternoon sun.

"My amulet."

"It's pretty," she said, her attention moving to his bandages.

His shoulder ached more than before, fresh blood seeping through the cloth of the dressing. Absorbed in his work, he hadn't paid much attention to the pain.

"I shouldn't have told you about this tree." Olyena shook her head. "You've re-opened your wounds."

Something in her tone made him pause and examine her emotions more closely.

An entirely new, pinkish glow inside her lured him in. Then he spotted the matching blush on her pale cheeks as her gaze slid down his bare torso.

"It'll be fine," he insisted, his own voice sounding a bit husky to his ear. "I'm not human, remember?"

She lifted his shirt off the ground and held it out to him.

"How could I forget," she muttered, then added a little louder, "Human or not, I can tell you're still hurting from your injuries."

The ever-present agony of hunger, much stronger than any physical pain, brought him closer to her. She pressed her hand with his shirt into his chest, avoiding his gaze now.

"Get dressed." Her voice was pleading. "It's still too cold this time of the year for prancing half-naked in the woods."

Making an effort not to snatch that tantalizing pinkish glow through the skin-to-skin contact of her hand on his chest, he rushed to skim it, barely able to wait until it slipped out of her.

Her interest in him, which clearly had a tint of sexual emotion for once, rushed over him with a shudder, coursing through his veins with intense pleasure and satisfaction.

"See?" She misunderstood. "You're shivering already. Put this on." She thrust his shirt into his hands then took a step back, away from him. "What's your name?" she asked unexpectedly, watching him pull his shirt on over his head. "I've never asked."

"Raim." He wiped off the sweat that had beaded on his forehead from the wood-cutting.

"Raim? Definitely not from this world." She grabbed the axe from the ground where he had tossed it. "Well, thank you for chopping all this wood. It will last me all the way until the summer, now. Come." She turned to go back to the cabin. "Dinnertime is soon. I still have some dried mushrooms left from last fall. I'll make some soup again."

"No luck with the traps?" Only now did he notice that her hands were empty of any game.

"No, not today. I've reset some of them. I'll go check again tomorrow."

They walked in silence for a few paces.

For the first time in his life, Raim did not need to worry where his next meal would come from. Having Olyena at his side staved off the agony of starvation that plagued all of his kind.

The realization that Olyena herself was basically starving churned in his gut, and he hated the feeling.

Raim knew very little about human food, and even less about the ways to find it. Personally, if he needed to procure anything, he approached it the way Incubi did when they required any supplies for the Base—they purchased them. Raim gave Olyena enough money to buy as much food as she wanted. Her obvious reluctance to use the gold for that purpose puzzled and even disturbed him.

"You know the gold I gave you would buy you a lot of meat," he brought it up again, carefully scanning her emotions. "No need to bother with the traps at all."

"To buy anything I'd need to find someone who would sell it to me," she muttered gruffly under her breath, but he heard her well enough.

"Wouldn't there be people willing to do that in the village?"

"Maybe."

Her replies made him only more confused, proving he knew nothing about interacting with humans, after all.

"What stops you then?" he asked directly. "I am well enough to stay on my own now, trust me—"

"I know," she cut him off abruptly. A flush of something dark inside her caught his attention.

"Why are you afraid of them?" he asked, venturing a guess.

"I'm not."

"I'll go with you," he offered on impulse. "Would that help?"

She took hold of the door handle as they arrived at her cabin.

"Watch the chickens," she mumbled, getting in.

"Olyena." Following her inside, he caught her by the arm and kicked the door closed. "What is it?"

"Nothing." She tried to free herself from his hold, but he flexed his fingers, not letting her flee his gaze either.

"You are scared to go to the village—"

"Not scared. Just . . . I'll do it later."

"I'll be gone later." In a few days, he should be well enough to get on his way back to the Base. "Would you rather go alone?"

"No . . ." She bit her bottom lip between her teeth.

"Let's go now, then. I'll come with you. Whatever it is that scares you—"

"Do you think you can protect me from all of them?" she challenged, finally meeting his eye straight on.

"You know I can." He held her gaze. "I'm much stronger than a human, remember?" He tilted his head in the direction of the wood piled outside of the cabin. Wood he had chopped using a flimsy axe and despite of having a number of serious injuries.

She freed her arm from him as he had loosened his grip. Taking a few steps back, she lowered herself onto a stool by the stove.

"They call me a witch," she said softly.

"But you're not—"

"Of course I am!" She glared at him. "I come from a family of witches. My grandmother was one. She just hid it well. They thought my mother was one, too. That's why they killed her."

"The villagers killed your mother?"

She nodded slowly. "They put her through the test of water, but she passed."

"What test?"

"You don't know?" She regarded him carefully. "Do you know anything at all about witchcraft?"

"The witchcraft you speak of is purely human imagination."

"It's not!" she protested with passion. "The water test is a real way to expose a witch. Everyone knows that. If you toss her into a deep water, the true witch will float. Her power would prevent her from drowning. The innocent will sink . . ." Her voice broke. "My mother drowned. She wasn't a witch. That's why they let my grandmother and me live. They thought we were innocent, too. Although, my grandmother already knew I had her gift . . . or her curse, as it may be."

"Were you there? When it happened?" He winced at the darkness spreading inside her from her memories, but his desire to learn more about her, to understand, would not let him stop the questions.

"I was small." Olyena diverted her gaze to the far wall, as if staring into the past. "But I remember. It was in the dead of winter. Freezing cold. They had to hack through the ice to get to the water in the river. Mother screamed when they shoved her in. Her red shawl floated on the surface long after her, but then it, too, sank . . ." Her lips trembled. "I've hated winter ever since. The water in the river freezes over, and I feel like she is trapped in there, in cold and darkness . . . She didn't have the magic to keep her afloat, not that it would have helped her. If she did float to the surface, they would have burned her as the witch. Then they probably would have done the same with grandmother and me. As it was, they drove us out of the village."

Her fear of people made perfect sense to him now.

"You're afraid they'd kill you, too?"

"I don't think they will now." Her voice didn't hold much certainty, though. "They need me. Grandmother taught me everything she knew—how to brew potions, heal wounds, make ointments, and birth a baby. I even know how to help a woman get pregnant with child, or prevent that from happening. Many come to see me whenever they need my help."

"But they don't want you in the village?"

"I don't want to be there, either," she scoffed, defiantly. "I'm fine where I am."

"Until you run out of food," he remarked, and she snapped a glare at him.

"Early spring is always tough. But it'll get better as it warms up."

"What are you going to eat until then?" he couldn't stop asking, finally recognizing the feeling that had been gnawing at him—*his* concern for *her*.

"I will be fine." She got up from the stool and started working on bringing the fire in the stove back to life. "This was not the first tough winter for me. Nor will it be the last. The summer will be here soon enough. The forest will have berries, nuts, and mushrooms that I can eat—"

"Until then, you'll be starving," he wouldn't let it go, he simply couldn't. Seeing her almost emaciated body disturbed him in more ways than he could explain. "With enough gold in your pocket to feed you like a queen for a year or even longer."

Her chest rose with another huff as she turned to set a pot of water over the stove.

"There is a market in the village in the summer," she said, her back to him. "Lots of people come from other places. I'll trade the gold then."

Raim considered her words for a moment. Having learned about the hostility of the villagers towards her, imagining Olyena going to that place on her own did not sit well with him.

"Is there anyone in the village who could trade you some food for your gold now?"

"Someone always *could*," she replied quietly. "The question is whether they *would*."

"Oh, they would," Raim promised. "I'll come with you. I can be very good at persuasion."

Chapter 9

A TWIG SNAPPED UNDER Raim's boot, sending a chipmunk dashing for cover from under their feet.

"Maybe I should set traps here," Olyena wondered out loud as the two of them walked through the forest towards the village. "I could empty them on the way back."

"On the way back you'll have no need to trap chipmunks, woman." Raim shook his head. "We're on our way to trade your gold and buy you food, remember?"

She nodded, although not with much conviction in the gesture.

"No one will touch you," Raim said, using the same firm voice he did when he had made his promise to her earlier.

Despite staying away from the heavy cloud of dark apprehension hanging over Olyena all morning, Raim could almost taste it, as if the putrid flavour was already burning his tongue.

"You know I won't let anyone hurt you." He swung his sword, chopping off a few branches of a hazelnut bush in their way. "They won't come near you unless you want them to."

"They won't need to come close to hurt," she replied, her voice barely audible, as she drew the grey rabbit-fur shawl tighter around her shoulders.

"They wouldn't dare," he assured her, although not entirely certain what exactly she meant.

She threw him a side glance, a smile ghosting her lips, probably at the sight of the eyepatch she had mastered for him from a piece of leather last night.

Raim couldn't understand a number of things from the past few days that he had spent one-on-one with a human. Right now, however, the most puzzling of these things was why the mission to get food for a woman he barely knew seemed so important to him.

He had much bigger plans and ambitions on his mind. The urgency to get on his way to return to the Base never left him. Still, he had delayed his departure, choosing to spend this day to serve as Olyena's guard, escorting her to the village.

She stumbled over a root in the ground, and he grabbed her elbow, steadying her. They had been trudging along the muddy forest floor since before sunrise. Olyena was definitely getting tired by now, and Raim made a mental note to buy a horse she could ride on the way back.

By the afternoon, the forest around them had thinned, the dark trunks of oak trees and occasional pines gradually replaced by the pristine white of birch trees.

"Not far now." Olyena gestured at the wide, open plain spreading out in front of them as they came to the edge of the forest. "Behind the river, just across the bridge."

Squinting with his one functioning eye, Raim could already make out the thin wisps of smoke from house chimneys against the pale sky.

"Well, let's go then." Sensing her tension, he took her hand in his, hoping that it would give her some reassurance.

It seemed to work. With a deep inhale, she squeezed his hand tight, then took a determined step towards the village.

THE WHISPERS WERE LOUD enough to reach him.

"The witch is here . . ."

"Has anyone invited her? What for?"

"What is she doing here?"

Raim knew Olyena heard them, too, as they walked along the main street. The grip of her hand on his was so tight, it nearly cut off his blood circulation.

"Who is that with her?" someone asked.

"A *leshy* from the swamp?" A woman giggled.

They were talking about him this time. Only the insult didn't offend him. *Leshy*—the old and ugly forest spirit—must still be a step above *nechistiy* since no one had attacked him with an axe yet.

"Here." Olyena stopped in front of the largest home on the street. With ornately carved wood trim and brightly painted window shutters, it was also the most remarkable one.

"This is where the blacksmith's cousin lives?" Raim rested his hand on the pommel of his sword at his hip.

Something in Olyena's emotions when she spoke of the blacksmith and his cousin, Kasimir, put him on guard. According to her, though, Kasimir was the richest man in the area. He traded regularly and was undoubtedly the one who had enough silver to break her gold into smaller, more usable for her, currency.

"Let's go then." He shoved at the gate with his shoulder, without knocking.

It seemed like the whole village had followed them here, curious faces peeking from every window and behind each fence. Raim had no doubt the occupants of Kasimir's house had been made aware of their visit, too, by now.

And indeed, as soon as he and Olyena set foot in the spacious fenced yard, a large male exited the house.

"What are you here for?" he asked, reproachfully, thumbs hooked in the richly embroidered belt under his sizeable belly—obviously the winter did not bring starvation to *his* house.

Olyena flinched under his stare, but then straightened her slim shoulders and took a step forward. "To trade."

"What do *you* have to offer?" The man asked, his expression bored. Something in his eyes though, as he slid his gaze along Olyena's figure, made Raim focus on the man's emotions more closely.

"I have gold," she replied firmly, holding her chin up.

"Gold? Where did you get it from?" With a flicker of interest flashing through his greed, the man threw a glimpse Raim's way.

Several people of every age and gender had spilled into the yard from the house by now. Even more entered from the street through the gate. A number of heads with curious expressions on their faces were peeking over the fence. At Kasimir's question, all of them openly ogled Raim.

Right now, the predominant feeling among the crowd was curiosity as they took in his eyepatch, his foreign clothing, and the unusual for this area colouring of his skin. Some trepidation and disgust mixed in whenever their stares landed on the ugly scars spreading from under the eyepatch over the left side of his face.

"It doesn't matter where I got my gold. What's important is that I'm willing to part with it." Olyena came closer to the man, who Raim had guessed must be Kasimir himself, and held out a coin on her palm. "I'll need to break this into silver, but I would also trade some for food. I'll take flour, spelt, oats, a half-dozen chickens—"

"Is it even real?" Kasimir grabbed the gold, lifting it to his face for inspection.

"Of course, it is."

"I'm not so sure." He squinted at the coin, bit into it, then raised it to his eyes.

A woman poked her head from around Kasimir's shoulder, tossing a curious glance Raim's way. She then focused her glare on Olyena.

"I can't believe you dared to show your face here," she bit out, huddling into a flowery wool shawl against the spring chill.

Olyena moved her gaze to the woman.

"Just returning your visit, Yaroslava," she replied calmly, even as Raim saw her emotions darken and churn.

"Shut your mouth," the woman hissed, but Kasimir had already perked up with attention.

"What do you mean?" He turned to the woman at his side. "Did you really go to see her? Why?"

"Don't listen to her." Yaroslava seemed to be ready to incinerate Olyena with her glare. "The witch is lying."

The atmosphere in the yard thickened, heavy with resentment towards Olyena.

Stretching his neck side to side, Raim stepped forward, placing himself between her and them. Hand on the handle of his sword, he pulled it out by about the length of his palm, letting the rays of the afternoon sun bounce off the curved Persian blade.

"Gold for food." He tipped his chin at the coin in Kasimir's hand. "It's a business transaction, nothing more."

"You see, I'm not sure I want to trade with her." Fisting the money, Kasimir rolled out his belly, placing hands on his hips in challenge. "What if I wanted to ask her some questions first?"

"Then you'll have to say goodbye to that coin." Raim came flush with the man. Keeping his attention on the emotions of the human, Raim was aware of the effect his gaze had on people when he searched inside them like that.

A shiver shuddered Kasimir's shoulders. The bravado and arrogance he had tried to pass for courage and confidence wavered under Raim's stare.

"Trade now," Raim said slowly, enunciating every word, "or we will leave."

The human blinked, his throat bobbed with a swallow. "What do you want for it?"

"Whatever she said." Raim released the man from the snare of his glare and stepped aside, bringing Olyena back in the view. Shoving the sword in, he kept his hand firmly on the handle. "Add a horse, too."

"Um, like I said . . ." Olyena cleared her throat. "Flour, chickens. A length of wool and one of linen, seven elbows each. Oats, butter, honey, too . . ."

Under Kasimir's orders, his household rushed to comply with Olyena's requests, piling up the goods in the yard, in front of her.

Feeling bored, Raim stood aside, watching the commotion and keeping an eye, still his only eye, on the overall atmosphere around Olyena. The hostility was still there, but it had subdued somewhat to the point that he could be fairly confident no one was planning to pounce on her or him.

"All done," Olyena exhaled, catching her breath.

The nerves, as well as the level of activity, must have sped up her breathing. Her cheeks blushed, and a dark strand had made its way out of her braid, falling over her face.

Raim swept his gaze over the yard, pausing it on the horse being led from the barn by one of Kasimir's helpers.

"We can leave," Olyena said quietly when the horse had been harnessed to a small open wagon now laden with food and other goods.

"As soon as you get your change." Raim nodded, moving his gaze back to Kasimir.

"It's fine, really . . ." Olyena tugged at his sleeve.

Raim assessed the wagon's content. He didn't know much about the value of the food. However, whatever knowledge he had gained about the value of the gold during his travels told him that what Olyena got must be below the value of the coin he gave her.

"Unless these chickens lay golden eggs, he owes you change." He glared at Kasimir.

Greed warred with fear in the human. His avaricious nature, however, didn't prove to be strong enough to combat the cowardice in him.

"Fine." Kasimir produced a thick purse from under his belt. "Here you go." He tossed a few silver coins Olyena's way.

They fell in the dust at her feet, and she quickly bent over to pick them up.

"You—" Raim pulled his sword out, lunging Kasimir's way. The disrespect this human showed to his hostess enraged him as if it had been against himself.

"Raim!" Olyena caught him by the arm.

Her grip would not have stopped him, but her voice did.

"It is a fair amount of change, Raim. Let's go. Please." She took the horse by the bridle, steering it from the yard while tugging Raim by his sleeve.

A glimpse at her emotions revealed the heavy unease inside her, convincing him to get her out of there as quickly as possible.

"Right." With one last glare of warning Kasimir's way, he followed her out.

Chapter 10

"ARE YOU SURE YOU DON'T want any?" Olyena asked Raim for probably the thousandth time, shoving a piece of pancake in her mouth.

It was the day after they had returned from the village. Olyena had since organized all the goods they brought back with them, making a stack of thin pancakes, with butter and honey, this morning.

Unable to tear his gaze away from the drop of honey that glistened on her bottom lip, Raim shook his head.

"No. I don't want to eat."

"How can anyone look at all this food and not want any?" She licked the drop off, and he found himself wondering about its taste. "It must be nice never to feel hungry." She sighed.

He quickly skimmed her contentment from the meal she just had. The emotion was pleasant but didn't have the sweetness he craved.

"Oh, I am hungry." His voice came out husky, prompting him to clear his throat. "Human food would do nothing to help me with that, though."

"You *are* hungry?" She shoved away the empty plate, giving him a confused look.

"Ravenously," he confessed.

Leaning across the small table, she stared at him, as if trying to read *his* emotions. "But not for the food I eat?"

"No." He pondered for a moment whether or not to tell her the truth. The temptation to be honest and see what came out of that proved too strong. "I sustain myself by using the energy of emotions from humans."

"How?" She frowned, though curiosity was still stronger in her than suspicion or fear, which he found encouraging.

"Like this." He skimmed it, knowing that it would reflect bright blue in his gaze directed at her.

"The lights? They mean you're feeding?" Understanding spread on her face, and he skimmed her satisfaction at that, too.

"Right."

"Did you just take my emotions? Without even touching me?"

"Yes."

"Hmm." Her frown deepened. "I didn't feel anything. It doesn't harm me in any way, does it?"

"No. I skim your emotions moments after you emit them. There is no harm that way."

For a few seconds she sat, staring at her hands folded on the table in front of her, probably thinking about his confession.

"I've been seeing these lights often of late." She met his gaze again. "You have been feeding all this time. Yet you're still hungry?"

"I have been feeding, but it's not enough." It was never enough. No matter what she would allow him to make her feel, the hunger would never leave, he knew that. Yet, the temptation to taste her desire gnawed at his insides almost as strong as the hunger itself.

"Well, can I help more, somehow?"

He scanned her emotions carefully, trying to assess how much he could tell her. After the trip to the village, her feelings for him had grown even warmer. The sense of comfort inside her shimmered peacefully in his company.

"For you to really help, I'll need you to *feel* something else," he ventured.

"Like what?"

He drew in a long breath. "Have you ever been touched, Olyena? By a man?"

Her contentment suddenly wavered and shrank. A dark shadow of pain and caution moved in inside her. "Why do you ask?"

Watching her emotions change, Raim felt something inside him drop, too. He loved the taste of the warm glow of comfort in her. Watching it vanish unsettled him more than he could have expected.

"You didn't enjoy his touch." He guessed the reason for her reaction.

Instead of replying, Olyena got up and started cleaning the dishes off the table.

"It can be done better," he rushed to assure her. "Much better."

She washed her plate, then put away the honey and butter—all without saying a single word. The darkness inside her thickened. Raim assumed her memories must be plunging her into sadness now. He wasn't sure what was the best way to clear the dark feelings away, but he longed for the return of that glow of comfort they had shared before.

"Who was he?" he asked, choosing the most direct way to purge it out of her—by lancing it with his question to expose and drain the pain and the darkness it brought.

"Does it matter?" She wiped her hands on her skirt. Gripping the back of the chair, she leaned on it, avoiding eye contact.

The uneven flutter of her emotions, like the wings of a wounded bird, made his insides twist. Shoving his chair back, he got up and closed the distance between them in one wide stride. Snapped from the darkness of her memories, Olyena recoiled at his sudden approach, but he caught her by her shoulders.

"It can be different." He held her gaze with his, trying to put the conviction he felt into his words. "Better. Truly enjoyable."

She tried to look away, but he made sure to hold her body and her attention firmly.

"Olyena. *I* can touch you the way a woman was meant to be touched."

Her eyes widened, chest rising faster. Then she shifted in his arms, pushing him away. "You're squeezing too tight, Raim," she snapped. "Right now, your touch hurts."

"I won't then." Hands up in a pacifying gesture, he retreated to the bed and sat down on the thin, straw-filled mattress. "I'm not going to touch you at all," he spoke carefully, afraid to drive her further away. "Let me just *tell* you what I would do if you allowed me to get close."

She remained standing by the chair, one hand resting on its back, but her body seemed to relax with the physical distance he had put between them.

"Tell me?" The dark turmoil inside her quieted a little under her undying curiosity, and Raim used the moment to proceed.

"If you ever let me touch you," he started. "I would be gentle." He kept her changing emotions in sight, gauging her reaction to his words.

It was different from feeding by touch, but not that much. He watched carefully what words would cause the most positive feeling in her, then built from there. "First, I'd brush the side of your face with the back of my fingers."

"Why the back?" She tilted her head as her interest flared.

"Because my palms are rough, calloused from every-day use. Right here . . ." he slid the tips of his left-hand fingers along the back of the ones on the right, "the skin is softer."

She followed his gesture with her gaze, her dark eyes glistening in the dim interior of the cabin.

"Then I would caress the side of your neck," he continued, not taking his focus off her emotions. "Most human men probably don't know it, but a woman's neck is a very sensitive part of her body—one of my favourite spots to touch, lick, and taste . . ."

He didn't remember the last time he actually physically touched a woman, if ever. His most intimate encounters with them happened when he furtively invaded their dreams to feed.

But he *knew* how he would touch Olyena if he was given that chance. He had always known.

Raim swallowed hard, as if he could already taste her skin—right there, in the soft spot between her neck and her shoulder where her sweet, feminine scent would be most intense.

"And then?" Olyena's throat moved with a swallow. Letting go of the chair's back, she plopped into it.

"Then I would kiss it," he half-whispered, bringing his voice down. "Right here." Lifting his hand, he touched his own neck, and she mirrored his gesture, stroking hers in exactly the same spot. Her eyes glazed over a bit.

"Because your lips are even softer than your fingers," she murmured.

"Exactly. I would stroke your arms, too. Right here." He tugged up the sleeve of his tunic, brushing his hand along the inside of his elbow and forearm. "And I know you would enjoy it—a woman's skin here is soft, silky, and extremely sensitive."

A small shudder ran across her shoulders as the warmest shade of orange flickered deep inside her. She rubbed her upper arm with her hand.

"You'd like my lips there even more," he rushed, eager to fan that tiny glow in her into something bigger. Sliding his gaze along her face, he paused it on her mouth, momentarily losing the trail of his thoughts.

Her lips parted. The bottom one, plump and fresh, teased him, tempting.

"Then I would want to kiss your mouth, too."

At his words, she pressed her hand to her lips.

"I'd suck your bottom lip between mine," he kept going, words rushing faster and faster out of him as his craving for her arousal grew. The more he got, the more he needed. "I'd taste you inside and out while I shove that linen shirt off your shoulders and take your breasts in my hands. Your nipples would be tender at first, the skin around them silky like rose petals, but they will grow hard under my fingers—tight and round—"

With a shuddered inhale, Olyena gasped, wrapping her arms around her, then jumped out of the chair, shoving it back with a screeching noise.

"Stop it." She stared at him wildly. The orange glow inside her was now streaked with blood-red. "No."

She dashed for the door.

"Olyena, wait!" He jumped off the bed.

"Don't follow me!" she yelled on her way out. "Don't you dare follow me!" She shut the door loudly, leaving him standing in the middle of the cabin.

Alone.

Chapter 11

LIFTING A LOG, RAIM fitted it over the one he had already placed, bringing the wall of the new chicken coup higher.

In a clipped voice and avoiding eye contact, Olyena had explained to him how she wanted it built before she left for the day.

'*To check the traps,*' she told him.

Although, with the food they had brought from the village a couple of days ago, she could very well have taken a break from trapping, hunting, and foraging in the woods for something to eat.

In his head, Raim went over the last real conversation they had—the day when he unleashed his fantasy in front of her—and wondered if he should have kept his mouth shut, instead.

Olyena had not been the same since. She talked little and wouldn't look him in the eye. What was worse, the warm glow of comfort he had grown to love in her had turned to grim tension whenever Raim was near now. The only thing that still gave him hope was a faint glimmer of red trying to break through the cloud of tension inside her. He was confident he could grow it into something more, something spectacular, if only she ever let him come close enough.

Making sure the log was secure, Raim picked up the axe and proceeded to clean the branches off another one. These logs were narrow and dense, cut from younger trees on the edge of the clearing. The way Olyena had designed it, the new chicken coup was to be constructed as a lean-to against the side of her cabin. She meant for it to be a place for the chickens to spend the day, but Raim had collected enough material to construct taller walls and a roof, too. This way the damn chickens could move out of the cabin and into their own place permanently. Since more of them had been brought from the village, there was hardly any place left for Olyena and him now.

Olyena and he.

Something warm and pleasant rose in his chest unexpectedly—Raim realized he liked the thought of them together like that.

Working with his hands, creating something he never would be able to had she not provided him with a design, also brought a sense of satisfaction he had never experienced before.

"This looks good." Olyena's soft voice snapped him out of his thoughts.

"Thank you." He pivoted on his heel to face her coming from behind the trees, a dead rabbit in her hands.

A swell of pleasure warmed his chest at the sight of her, or maybe it was the resonance of *her* pleasure he had skimmed as she approached.

"We'll have a stew tonight." She lifted the game up for him to see. "Well, *I* will. You'll just . . . watch me eat," she added grimly, moving her gaze away quickly. It landed on the partially-completed chicken coup again. "It's bigger than I expected." She pointed at the newly-constructed wall.

"I figured I'd enclose it from all sides, so the fox wouldn't get in at night."

"You want them to stay in there overnight?"

"Yes, starting today, actually. I really prefer not to spend another night with the birds running all over me."

She smiled. "They sleep at night, they don't run. Well, maybe a little, early in the morning."

"Even 'a little' is more than I'm willing to put up with." He lifted the panel he had put together from the split logs and placed it on top of the walls. "This is the roof, see? I'll attach it temporarily for tonight, but I'll have to firm it up tomorrow. There is not enough daylight left to finish it properly today."

"You got a lot done, Raim. You have basically built the whole thing in one day."

"I don't get tired," he reminded. "Don't need to take meal breaks, either."

"About that . . ." She placed the rabbit on the pile of logs then sat on a cut tree stump nearby. "I shall tell you. I don't think I want to feel the things you need me to feel in order to feed you."

Sharp pang of disappointment cut through him at the prospect of losing any chance to coax out the desire he had glimpsed in her. After getting that one tiny tease of a taste of her arousal, he had been fantasizing about more ever since.

"You don't have to feed me that way, Olyena." He hid his disappointment, keeping busy by securing the roof over the chicken coup and making sure it would stay put for the night.

The dark trepidation in her worried him.

"I would love to. I really would," she said, and the longing in her voice squeezed around his heart.

On one hand, he yearned to make her feel all the wonderful things he knew he could create for her. It physically pained him that fear prevented her from unleashing her desire. He knew how much pleasure women were capable of feeling, and he wanted that experience for Olyena.

At the same time, he knew well enough that emotions like that could not be rushed or forced.

That must have been the problem—someone obviously had forced that on her before, scarring her for life now.

". . .but I don't think I could." She stared at the ground between her feet.

"Tell me," he prompted, holding his breath in anticipation.

For one long moment, it seemed she would push him away, once again.

Then she actually started speaking.

"There were three of them," she kept her gaze down. "They were hunting in the woods, further north from here." She waved her hand in that direction. "I tried to hide, but it was too late. They spotted me through the trees. I ran, but they caught me . . ."

The raw pain spilling in a muddy gush out of her made his breath hitch. His chest filled with an emotion he had hardly ever felt before—compassion.

Then the much more familiar rage stirred.

"What did they do?" Aggression rose to the surface, demanding action from him. His fingers twitched, itching to snap the necks of her abusers. "Who were they?"

She glanced up at him. "You are a good man, Raim—probably because you are *not* a man. Most people I know are not nice at all, and only a handful are tolerable."

The gravity in her voice, her grim expression—both seemed too dark and heavy for her age. His rage fizzled under his concern for her, which felt more important at the moment. Instead of murdering someone, more than anything in the world he longed to ease her pain.

He wished he knew more about how to give comfort, but he tried anyway.

"Forget about them," he said, even as he guessed that forgetting probably wouldn't be easy. "They are not worth any of this, sweetheart." Kneeling in front of her, he smoothed her long hair out of her face then brushed away a tiny little tear dangling off her lower eyelid. "They have no idea, no understanding at all."

He wondered how the males of her own species could have so little knowledge about their own females. True, they didn't rely on a woman's sexual energy to feed. Was that why most of them remained utterly ignorant about the many ways to bring their women pleasure?

Staring at the hurricane of pain churning in Olyena's eyes, Raim wished to make her feel better, to help her forget what she didn't want to remember.

She touched lightly the deep, healing scars criss-crossing his face, the focus of her expression sharpening. "You were very handsome, Raim, before this injury, I can tell now. Even with the scars . . ." Her voice trailed off as her fingers continued to explore his face, first tracing the puckered, healing skin of his wounds, then touching his temple, and skimming the line of his jaw covered by a several-days-old beard. "You also make me feel . . . so many different things. But fear is no longer one of them. When you're here, I'm not afraid. And I really don't remember a day in my life when I wasn't scared of something or someone before you came along."

A shimmering haze rose deep inside her, and he stilled, afraid that even the slightest movement would spook it away like a fleeing butter-fly.

Her gaze stopped on his mouth as she lightly brushed his bottom lip with the pad of her thumb.

"Not all touch has to be painful," she whispered, almost to herself. "That's what you said, right?"

"Right," he exhaled, swaying closer to her.

"How do I know it won't turn that way? Even if it starts gentle?"

"Because I give you my promise."

"Why would you?"

"Because I would hate to see you hurt."

"Why do you care?"

"I have no idea."

That was true. Raim didn't know exactly the reasons for this new tenderness he had for Olyena. No human had ever caused him to feel that way. But then again, she was the only human he had ever allowed to come close, and not just physically. She had been his sole source of nourishment for over a week now. Her emotions had been *his* all this time. Any pain felt by her seemed to now have the ability to hurt him deeply, too.

"What I do know is that I'd rather lose my only eye than harm you in any way," he said sincerely.

A tiny smile curved her lips, bringing his focus to her mouth.

"You have no idea how good that sounds." She inhaled deeply, then said softly, "Put your hands behind your belt."

Her request surprised him, but he obeyed, sliding his fingers under the leather of his belt.

"Keep them there," she whispered, leaning in.

Her warm, fresh breath fanned across his face, making his skin tingle with an unknown sensation. Then her lips brushed by his, and his heart all but stopped.

He didn't need to read her emotions to sense her hesitation. Her caress was barely there, not much stronger than the brush of a butterfly wing. But that slight contact shook him to his very core.

Until now, all he ever focused on was how his touch affected the emotions of the woman he fed off. Never before during a feeding had he thought about how being with her affected *him*. Olyena's kiss flooded him with sensations all of his own.

"Did I do it wrong?" Her voice filtered through the sweet dizziness enveloping him head to toe.

"There is nothing wrong with anything you do . . ." he rasped.

He realized he had disobeyed her order and removed his hands from under his belt only when he wrapped his arms around her waist, bringing her closer. She didn't seem to mind though, leaning into his body, too.

"Kiss me, Raim," she begged against his mouth. "Kiss me like you said you would."

A groan vibrated through his whole being when he took her mouth with his. Sucking on that plump, soft bottom lip that had invaded his thoughts, he let himself get lost in her taste. Inside and out.

Her arousal flooded him, awakening every nerve in his body. The whole world seemed to fall out of existence as he sank deeper and deeper into the tantalizing cloud of Olyena's emotions. He was skimming and taking at random, greedily drinking as much as he could, mindful only of staying away from her life force at all cost.

With a soft moan, she pressed herself to him, raking her fingers through his hair. The elusive red streak pulsed inside her, and he zoomed in on it, longing for it to grow. Sliding his hands up her sides, he cupped her nape with one, searching with the other for the way under her coat.

She broke the kiss off suddenly, but didn't pull away completely. Moving her hands to his shoulders, she leaned her forehead to his, breathing hard.

"That was . . . intense, Raim."

Concerned, he scanned her emotions hurriedly. They were a tangled mess, but a beautiful one. Excitement, curiosity, and joy—all intertwined with that thin but bright red ribbon of lust. The faint, silver shadow of trepidation was what must have made her break the kiss, he guessed.

"I—I just need to catch my breath," she panted. "Being with you brings so many feelings at once."

That was exactly how he felt about her.

"Let's go make that stew then?" He kissed the side of her face. "We'll have plenty of time later."

Only how much time was he actually planning to stay in these woods with her?

Rising to his feet, Raim helped Olyena up, banishing the annoying question away to some dark abyss deep in his mind.

Chapter 12

TOGETHER, THEY MOVED the chickens to the newly-constructed coup, then cleaned the rabbit that Olyena had trapped. Afterwards, she swept the floors in the cabin and made dinner.

She had left the wooden shutters open on the glassless window, and the fresh spring air mingled with the pleasant warm smell of the stew on the stove. Raim saw her contentment again, skimming it constantly.

After she finished eating her dinner and did the dishes, she sat at the table across from him, with a spoonful of honey for dessert.

"Where exactly did you come from, Raim?" Olyena asked unexpectedly. "Where will you go once you leave here?"

Leave.

It took him a moment to focus on the word enough to fully grasp its meaning. Being here with her, he didn't want to think about any other place out there at all.

"Um, I'll be going South. To join the rest of my kind at our Base in the Empire. That's where we live."

"You're not really a forest spirit then, right?" She took some honey from the spoon, and he watched her pink tongue dart to lick it off her lips. "What are you?"

"I am an Incubus."

"Incubus? What is that?"

"A demon."

She nodded thoughtfully, not demanding a more detailed explanation.

"There are all possible kinds of beings in this world," she said. "My mother is a water nymph now—a *rusalka*. I talk to her whenever I go to the river."

Raim had never met anyone other than humans and demons in this world. To his knowledge, there wasn't anyone else. But who was to say that for sure? In any case, Olyena's beliefs helped her accept him for what he was—someone other than herself—and he felt grateful for that.

"Your injuries are healing well," she observed, her emotions dimmed inside her somewhat. "When are you planning on leaving?"

Her question brought his thoughts back to leaving again. And again, he didn't feel like thinking or talking about it.

"I haven't decided yet."

Truthfully, there was nothing that held him here at this point. He could see perfectly fine now, although still only from one eye. Thanks to Olyena, he had enough energy to make it to the next village on his way to the Empire and his Base. He didn't even need to feel any guilt about leaving her—she had enough food for now, and he would leave her all his remaining gold that she could trade in at the summer market for years to come.

Yet, the thought of parting with Olyena brought up only unpleasant emotions in him. Even the prospect of the Grand Master position no longer seemed that appealing. Why go through the trouble of taking over the humans and filling the Base with them if he could be this easily satisfied simply by being with one of them?

"You are welcome to stay for as long as you want," she offered. "I like having you here. It feels safe with you." She put the spoon down, keeping her eyes on it. "Would you . . . um, like to feed now, too?"

"Me?"

It took him a moment to realize she was not referring to the honey or the stew. The tender pink of expectation fluttered inside her like a silk scarf in the wind.

"I mean if that kiss was any good for you . . ." she trailed off for a moment before finishing in a single rushed breath, "I would not be against another one like that."

Understanding spread like warm melted butter through his insides. Leaning back, he draped his arm over the back of his chair, restraining himself from pouncing on her too hard in his eagerness.

"A kiss?"

"Mmhm." She nodded quickly, keeping her eyes on her hands. A delicate blush glowing on her cheeks made him want to kiss her entire face, without delay, but he lingered, denying himself the immediate pleasure.

"What if I end up doing more than kissing?"

"You might?" She shot her gaze up to his. "Like what?"

The trepidation in her had a very strong tint of excited anticipation, so he continued. "I want to touch more of you." He got off his chair and stepped around the table to her.

"More?" she whispered, getting up, too. His chest was at her eye level now, and that was where she stared.

"I want to *see* more of your body, too." He forced his hands to remain at his sides, waiting for just the right moment. "Naked."

"You want me to . . . undress?" A sharp spike of alarm shot through her.

"Or let *me* undress you," he said quickly, making his voice sound soft and soothing, enthralling, not threatening. "Which one would you prefer?"

Thankfully, the needle of panic inside her melted into nothing once he had given her the choice. The flare of excitement sparked brighter.

Her gaze still somewhere in the area of his chest, she slowly lifted her hands. With trembling fingers, she untied the rope she used for a belt. The ends of the long wool vest she wore over her linen tunic fell open. Slowly, so very slowly, she slid the vest off her shoulders and dropped it on the chair behind her, without so much as a glance at where it fell.

"More?" Her whisper barely reached his ear.

"Yes." He fisted his hands, impatiently. The teasing wisps of her timid excitement served as an appetiser, wetting his craving for more.

Her hands at her back, she untied the laces holding her skirt around her waist. The heavy material dropped to her feet, leaving her standing in nothing but the long linen shirt.

The orange and burgundy of the dying sunset danced in her hair, along with the glow of the fire in the stove—all mixing with the warm colours of her emotions.

"You do the rest," she said softly, her voice a little more steady now.

He didn't need a clarification this time. Closing the distance between them, he fought the urge to rip the shirt off her. Instead, he lifted his hand to her face, stroking the side of it with his knuckles.

She trembled at the contact, but didn't move away.

"Now the neck?" She guided him with her question.

Brushing her hair aside, he caressed the side of her neck—his favourite spot on a woman. He loved the feeling of building anticipation that touching it brought. It always held the promise of more.

Sliding his finger along the delicate column of her throat, he lifted her chin up, forcing her to face him. "How about a kiss now?"

She parted her lips in reply, ready for him.

He glided the tip of his tongue along her lip first, tasting the honey, then deepened the kiss, claiming her mouth exactly how he now knew she liked.

She moaned when his tongue brushed by hers, a shimmering wave of anticipation rolling through her emotions along with a shudder running through her body.

Moving his hands down her shoulders, he shoved the shirt off her. Wide and shapeless, it pooled around her feet at once, baring her for him.

Her pale skin seemed even lighter in contrast with her black hair. Wrapped in the glow of the fire, she seemed so much more than a mere human to him. He might have fallen from Heaven, but *she* appeared to have so much more of the Divine at that moment.

"Angel . . ." he whispered, untying the ribbon holding her braid. The silky strands sprang loose under his fingers, and he raked his hands through the heavy mass.

Rising on her toes, she reached for another kiss, taking his mouth herself this time, and he surrendered to the feeling of absolute delight this gesture brought.

He found her breast with his hand, the nipple already hard from the chill from the window.

"Should I close the shutters now?" he asked, between kisses.

"No." She fisted her fingers into his tunic. "Don't leave."

Arms around her waist, he walked her backwards towards the bed, all the while kissing her face.

His control had slipped. Greed and hunger prevented him from executing each and every kiss as perfectly as he would have liked. She didn't seem to mind, though, her body softened and slackened under his messy display of affection. Whatever apprehension had still lingered inside her had melted away.

He kicked his boots off, but didn't bother with the rest of his clothes as he lowered her onto the bed, getting in next to her. She lifted her arms over her head, stretching on the bedding, and he stroked the insides of her arms with his hands, watching the tiny sparks of pleasure twinkle in the wake of his touch.

Kissing down her body, he savored the taste of her skin—an intoxicating cocktail when mixed with the tantalizing flavours of her emotions. Sucking on her nipple, he felt her rock her hips against his thigh, then saw the red flare inside her pulse brighter.

Now.

Gliding his hand down, he slid his finger between her legs, then swallowed her gasp of alarm with another kiss. She stilled for a moment when he found the spot that made women moan and writhe when he rubbed it in their dreams. But this was the first time he ever physically touched a woman this intimately in real life.

The sharp spike of crimson passion inside Olyena when he pressed on that spot with the pad of his thumb tasted like nothing he had ever fed on before. Sweet, just like the honey of her kiss, and so filling, he almost believed his hunger could be satisfied for once.

"More," she panted, lifting her hips to meet his hand. "Oh yes, right there . . . more please."

Moving over her, he slid his finger inside her, then spread the sleek warmth seeping out between her folds, rubbing harder where she wanted him to.

Her moans grew louder, her breathing came out in bursts of air until he sensed the very moment she came undone. He captured her mouth in a biting kiss, swallowing the screams of her bliss as she shuddered through her orgasm under him.

The intense, heady satisfaction of her release flooded him from the inside. His arms shook, and he dropped at her side, moving his hand to cup the curve of her hip.

She rolled to her side right away, gripping the tunic on his chest. Her eyes closed, she pressed her forehead between her hands.

"What just happened, Raim . . .?" she whispered. "It couldn't have been of this world."

"Oh, it very much was, my sweet." He kissed the top of her head, pulling the cover over her flushed body to shield her from the evening chill. "Every feeling and emotion you just had came from you," he assured her, adding, "This is one of the best things about this world, actually. If not the best one of all."

Chapter 13

SPRING WAS GAINING strength, bringing more light and warmth with it. Raim's days were filled with light, too. Lying in bed, waiting for the sun to rise each morning, he listened to the soft breathing of the sleeping Olyena at his side, wishing for nothing more.

His plans and his ambitions had somehow moved to the background as he kept convincing himself there was still plenty of time to make it to the Base before the election.

One day, he would get on his way. Maybe tomorrow, maybe next week . . .

Meanwhile, he stayed with her.

Through the day, he helped Olyena with whatever chores needed to be done around the house. He went to the creek to fetch water with her, and deeper into the woods to set and empty the traps.

At night, Raim learned the many delightful ways to play Olyena's body to satisfy them both. The hunger that had been ruling his life had decreased to a faint shadow of itself by now. Some days, he hardly noticed it at all.

About a week or two after the evening she first bared herself to him, he took his shirt off before going to bed. With the nights getting warmer, the layer of clothing made him uncomfortably warm lately.

"I've noticed this before, when I treated your wounds." Olyena fingered the leather cord around his neck. "And later when you cut the wood. Where did you get it?"

"My amulet?" He slid his fingers down the cord to the polished, teardrop shaped stone on it. "I had it carved from a cross a monk once used to try banishing a demon out of me." He chuckled. "That didn't work of course, he didn't know that the demon *was* me. I sent him running but kept the cross as a souvenir."

"Is it on fire?" Propped on an elbow, she touched the stone lightly. "It's glowing."

Lying on his side next to her, he traced the worried wrinkle on her forehead, wishing it would go away, along with any shadow of concern inside her. "It's because of me. The cross was carved from *soros* stone. Monks use it to find us. The stone came from the same world I did, and it glows when one of our kind is near."

"Why do you wear it? It gives you away." She gazed at him, inquisitively.

"It reminds me of who I am."

"But it tells those who hunt you who you are, too."

"I'm not afraid of them." He flexed his fingers, inclosing the amulet into his fist.

"You're not afraid of anyone and anything," she stated, confidently.

"Well, there are some things . . ."

"Like what?"

"I'm afraid I'll have to stop talking now."

"Why?"

"Because I really want to kiss you," he murmured, leaning in and doing just that.

The readiness with which she met his kiss thrilled him. The timid insecurity of before was all but gone by now. After days of touching and kissing between them, Olyena's confidence had grown. Sliding her palms up and down his skin, she explored his body the same way he had been exploring hers.

Her caress created sensations in Raim he wasn't sure how to deal with. It brought to the surface the echoes of her best emotions inside him, making him feel as if they were also his own. Pleasure spread through his chest in ripples, radiating through the rest of his body.

Moaning against his mouth, Olyena arched her back, pressing herself against him. Her leg bent, she slid her thigh between his. Her hands travelling down his back and slipping under the waistband of his pants, she cupped his backside to draw him closer to her.

Heat ran up the insides of his thighs, pooling in his groin with a throbbing pressure that begged to be released.

"What do you want *me* to do?" Olyena's whisper fanned across his lips, swollen hot after their kiss. "What can I do to bring *you* pleasure?"

Her hand inside his pants moved to the front. His body seemed to reach out to her of its own accord. The power of her pull shocked him.

'You're not afraid of anyone and anything.'

Raim realized there *was* something that terrified him, after all—the amount of power this woman managed to acquire over him during the few short weeks they had spent together.

Jerking back, away from her touch, he caught her hand by the wrist.

"What's wrong?" she whispered, and he could barely stand the grey that shaded her emotions.

"Nothing, my sweet." He kissed her forehead, her temple, the ridge of her cheekbone . . . Bringing her hand to his lips, he kissed it too. "Nothing is wrong."

He trailed his kisses down her body, savoring the familiar taste of her skin and lust mixed into one.

Shifting down along her body, he covered every inch of her with kisses until she writhed and moaned, wrapped into the crimson passion of her desire. "Remember? My lips are softer than my hand."

She tensed, alarmed, when he parted her knees. "Even there?"

"Especially here," he assured her, dipping his head between her thighs.

His confidence returned to him as he made her moan louder, skimming every red tendril of her arousal. His world seemed to have found its balance once again. Swirling his tongue around Olyena's most sensitive spot as she shuddered with the orgasm he gave her, Raim fed off it all.

"Don't ever leave me, Raim . . ." she murmured sleepily afterwards, snuggling into his side. "Stay here, with me. Always."

LYING IN THE DARKNESS of the cabin—Olyena curled against his chest—Raim longed for the true and familiar sense of contentment, which had escaped him tonight.

'*Stay,*' she had said. And everything in him wanted to obey her call.

Over time, Olyena had become his home, his beacon—the woman whose requests he longed to fulfill.

An ordinary human, whose orders he was unable to disobey.

The thought sent dreadful chill up his spine.

They had closed the shutters for the night. The soft amber glow of the pendant on the cord around his neck was the only source of light inside now.

He mechanically moved his hand to the *soros* stone, wrapping his fingers around the familiar smooth surface, warm with the heat of his body.

'*It reminds me of who I am.*'

Except that he had forgotten it lately. Wrapped in Olyena's soft body and tantalizing emotions, he had forsaken everything.

Gremory was out there, maybe still in need of help. Incubi had often been burnt, decapitated or maimed when captured. What if Gremory was being tortured this very moment as he lay cuddling with a human in here?

The Council election was but months away. There was still a lot to do for Raim to have a shot at the position of Grand Master. Yet, here he was—softened by a female, lured in by her emotions that seemed to be incredibly potent to combat the Incubi hunger, but at a price.

He had been weakened.

By a mere mortal . . .

Raim's chest tightened with longing, so intense it seemed able to tear him apart. Only, he no longer was capable of telling who or what this feeling was for—the woman at his side or the loyalty to his kind that, until now, had governed all his actions.

Carefully, so as not to disturb her sleep, he freed himself from Olyena's embrace. Avoiding so much as a glance at her, he rose from the bed. His mind, however, immediately supplied the image of Olyena in slumber. He'd watched her asleep enough times for the picture to firmly embed itself in his brain.

Soft, warm, her hand under her cheek, she would curl into a ball like a kitten, as if making herself smaller helped her feel more secure in her most vulnerable state. Only when they started sharing the bed, did she uncurl, stretching herself along his side, as if wanting to touch as much of him as possible during the night.

Getting dressed quickly, he held the scabbard with the sword in his hand for a moment, then placed it on the table. Leaving it was a pathetic attempt to protect her, even if he was no longer physically with her. Before opening the door outside, he took off his amulet, too, and put it next to the sword. This was just an impulse that he had no desire to analyze.

Shoving the door open, Raim left the cabin, without saying goodbye.

He couldn't possibly wait for when she awoke. If he faced her, he knew he would bow to her will and stay with her for the rest of her life, forsaking all others. And when she would be inevitably gone, in a few short decades—all humans died, sooner or later—there was simply no way of telling what he would become then or how he would be able to face the rest of eternity, without her.

Instead, he fled in the middle of the night, like a coward, while she slept.

Olyena was wrong, there absolutely *were* things he was afraid of. And she was the biggest one of them.

Chapter 14

FOR ONCE IN HIS LIFE the pain of hunger was not the most excruciating thing for Raim to bear. Every step he took away from the small cabin in the woods and from the woman peacefully sleeping in it twisted in his chest with agony.

Her energy was strong and potent inside him, making him feel he could make it all the way to the Empire without having to stop once.

Yet not knowing how to bear this pain all the way to the Base, he took a turn East, heading in the direction of the village first.

"GET UP," RAIM SQUEEZED through his teeth, grabbing the sleeping man by the scruff of his shirt and pulling him out from under the down-filled cover.

The purpose of Raim's visiting a human dwelling this time was not to invade people's dreams but to yank them out of them.

"What . . . Who? How dare you!" Kasimir staggered to his feet, wildly blinking the remnants of sleep away.

"Who else was with you that day?" Not loosening his hold, Raim gave him a hard shake.

A high-pitched shriek cut through the air from the other side of the bed. "Who is that, Kasimir?" Kicking her feet, the woman scooted all the way to the headboard, cowering under the thick, puffy quilt.

"Get your hands off me!" Kasimir batted at Raim's arm holding him. "I swear I'll get your head chopped off this time, you filthy witch-fucker."

"I'll be the one doing the chopping tonight," Raim gritted through his teeth, dragging the struggling and kicking man out of the bedroom and to the front door.

Another high-pitched wail came from the narrow bed placed by the large river-rock stove. "Oh, good people, what is happening!" The wrinkled face of an elderly female peeked from around the stove as she screamed at the top of her lungs.

"Dragged out from his own bed!" Kasimir's woman rushed out of the bedroom, wrapping a large colourful shawl around her shoulders as a number of other people, male and female, staggered into the common room from all possible nooks and crannies inside the house. "By this *leshy* here!" The woman pointed at Raim with both hands.

Ignoring the noise and commotion, he kicked the front door open, shoving Kasimir into the yard. The rising sun had barely touched the edge of the dark sky. Raim had marched through the night, covering the distance to the village considerably faster this time.

With a last glance around the room, Raim swiped a large butcher knife off the table then walked outside, towards Kasimir.

"Who else was with the witch that day?" he demanded, grabbing the man by the throat and shoving the knife under his nose. "She said there were three."

It had taken him awhile to figure out that Kasimir must have been involved in what happened to Olyena that day in the woods. Unfamiliar with interactions between humans, Raim didn't immediately interpret the signs the day he came to the village with Olyena to trade her gold. The emotions he spotted in both in reaction to each other—especially Olyena's paralyzing fear and resentment towards this man—only started to make sense when he went through them after leaving the cabin earlier tonight.

Then the certainty had settled in—and with it a blinding rage rose.

"Who else was there," he hissed, shoving the blade until a thin trickle of blood squeezed from the human's skin, dripping down Kasimir's lip and into his mouth.

The inherent arrogance of the human turned to genuine fear the moment he tasted his own blood.

"Stoyan . . ." he sputtered the name.

"Who?"

"Stoyan, my cousin, the blacksmith . . ."

"And? The third one?"

"Ratco, his brother-in-law—"

"Lead me to their houses."

"They live in the same one. Stoyan is yet unmarried."

"How convenient." Raim grabbed the scruff of Kasimir's shirt again. "Lead!" He shoved the man ahead of him.

Tripping down the street, Kasimir kept blubbering, "Listen, what's in it for you? Let me go. I'll pay you. I'll give you the gold she traded and more."

Raim ignored his whining, prodding him with his knee to his side. "Where to, now?"

The human meekly gestured at another large house, a few doors down from his.

The lights were on inside, the narrow strips of it filtered through the cracks between the wood shutters, fighting the greying sunrise.

Someone rushed Raim with a pitchfork the minute he kicked in the door. Leaping back a step, Raim let the teeth of the pitchfork embed into the wood of the door, then ripped the handle out of the hands of the man who had attacked him.

Tossing Kasimir to the floor, he pointed his new weapon at his attacker.

"Stoyan?"

"No . . ." he muttered, weakly.

"I'm Stoyan." A tall, broad man stepped into the lit area in the middle of the common room. "Leave my in-law alone, outsider."

The sudden thought of how much larger the male was compared to Olyena's frail shape made Raim's insides churn. He swayed on his feet from the sickening feeling.

"This here is Ratco then?" he bit out, diverting his attention to the one who had attacked him with the pitchfork.

Thinking of Olyena made Raim weak in the knees. He called on his rage again, using it as a shield and a weapon.

The shorter man grabbed on to the teeth of the pitchfork Raim pointed at him, as if hoping to stop them from piercing through him. He nodded quickly. "I'm Ratco . . . What do you want?"

"I want all three of you." Keeping his glare on Stoyan, Raim grabbed Kasimir by his throat again.

"You should have heard her moans and screams," the human in his grip croaked in protest. "I swear she liked it—"

Raim's fingers tensed, cutting the man's air supply off. With an effort, he forced them to relax a bit, lest he kill Kasimir at once—too easy a death for him.

"Out." He shoved him back into the yard.

Just like Kasimir's house, this place had been filling with people way too quickly for Raim's comfort. He needed an open space to minimize the risk of a sudden attack. He had to keep a distance from all of them, except for these three.

Ratco didn't make him say it twice. Whimpering, with his gaze fixed on the pitchfork, he scurried to the door. Raim caught him by the shirt before he escaped.

"You too," he ordered Stoyan, who crossed his arms over his chest, glaring back at him defiantly.

Raim cursed under his breath, without letting go of Ratco, he dropped the pitchfork and grabbed Stoyan by his shirt. The larger male staggered with a strangled noise of surprise as Raim shoved him to the door, not holding back his strength. The linen ripped in his fingers when Stoyan dug his feet into the floorboards, trying to resist.

With another filthy curse of barely contained rage, Raim seized Stoyan's arm and tossed the male out of the door.

Stoyan brayed like a mule when he hit the ground, then rolled in the dust clutching his now dislocated arm.

Kasimir crouched on the ground when Raim stepped into the yard, dragging Ratco behind him and holding the butcher's knife in his other hand.

"Go away!" Kasimir sobbed, attempting to escape on all fours. "I swear I'll never come near that bitch ever again."

"I know you won't." Tossing Ratco aside, Raim hooked the toe of his boot under Kasimir's ribs, rolling him to his back. "I'll make sure of it."

He knelt by the blubbering man, pressing him into the dirt with one hand against his chest. "I'm the one doing the chopping tonight," he reminded. Lifting the hem of Kasimir's shirt with the tip of the blade, Raim shoved the man's knees apart with his boot and sliced the human's shrivelled cock off before he could peep a word of protest.

It happened too fast for anyone to prevent it. Yet as soon as the blood gushed into the dust of the yard floor, and Kasimir's wild bellowing ripped through the early morning, the whole village seemed to come to life.

Someone from the stable area tossed an axe at Raim. He caught it in the air, leaping to his feet.

With a growl, Stoyan rushed him. Gaze unhinged, injured arm cradled to his side with the other one, he lunged at Raim, aiming to ram him, to crush him with the sheer force of his body mass and his rage.

Raim's own anger ran ice cold, and therefore was more deadly. Stepping out of Stoyan's way, he swung the axe, chopping off the man's injured arm and sending him to his knees.

With a deafening roar, the wounded man hit the ground, clutching his bleeding stump, and rolled in the dirt that was quickly soaked with his blood.

The air erupted in screams, people rushing to the injured men on the ground, women wailing, children starting to cry somewhere in the distance.

Ignoring it all, Raim focused on one noise out of the cacophony of thousands—the panicky bellowing of Ratco as he dashed for the gate in a clear attempt to escape the fate Raim had come to bestow upon him.

"Pathetic human," Raim grunted, leaning back before tossing the axe Ratco's way. The weapon turned and twisted through the air, but the blade sunk in just the way Raim had intended—deep and clean, cracking the man's head in two all the way to the base of his neck.

"You demon! Be you cursed forever!" Kasimir's woman cried, dropping into the dust at her husband's side. "Look what you've done to him."

Pressing both hands to his crotch, blood soaking his shirt, Kasimir howled in pain, his high screams intermingling with strangled groans.

"Judging by his moans and screams," Raim replied calmly, "I'd say he likes it."

Tossing the knife into the dirt at her feet, he turned to leave, but someone else leaped at him, swinging a fist at him.

Trying to defeat a demon with his bare hands.

What a fool.

Raim caught the man's arms, squeezing his wrists as he stared into his eyes. Reaching deep inside, he never even bothered with the man's many emotions. Instead, he searched for his life force, draining it at once as soon as he found it.

Lifeless, the man's body hung limply in Raim's hands before he let it go, dropping the corpse at his feet.

He swept the yard with his gaze then, pausing it on the terrified faces of the onlookers.

"The woman in the woods is your goddess," he addressed them all. "Worship her, protect her from cold, hunger, and outsiders, lest I return and make your heads roll."

"Filthy, pathetic humans," he muttered under his breath in disgust, as he made it along the street and into the valley, past the last dwelling of the settlement and the tall fence that surrounded it.

The excruciating pain that had wrecked him since the moment he left Olyena's bed was still there. Only now he believed he had brought it under control by drowning it in a river of blood.

Chapter 15

OLYENA

She woke up to the familiar sounds of the forest outside and the commotion of the chickens in the lean-to coup. Before the awareness of the reality fully returned to her, she stretched, patting the mattress next to her, then stilled as the feeling of loss sliced through her anew.

He was gone.

It'd been a week since that morning when she first discovered that Raim had left her—in the middle of the night, without even saying goodbye, just when she started to hope he might never leave at all.

All of that hurt, but finding herself alone again, after she had tasted the comfort and safety of having someone in her life, hurt the most.

A scurrying noise and some muffled voices on the other side of her door caught her attention. They didn't terrify her the way they did the first time she heard them, the day after Raim left.

Fighting the all-consuming sadness that threatened to overtake her, Olyena lowered her feet to the dirt floor and grabbed the piece of wool fabric she used for a shawl. Wrapping it around her shoulders, she padded to the door.

A large basket waited for her on the other side—a loaf of bread, a clay pot of butter or maybe sour cream tied with a piece of cloth, some root vegetables, and even a coil of sausage were in it.

As she had expected, no one was around. Only the sound of rustling in the undergrowth in the distance revealed the direction in which her secret providers were departing.

"Thank you!" She yelled towards the noise then heaved the basket as the rustling faded into the trees. Whoever delivered the offering clearly was not interested in having a conversation.

Fingering the cloth on the butter pot, she recognized the weave of it. The material was identical to the one she had traded for in the village last time to make a tunic for herself. The goodies in the basket definitely came from the village.

Olyena didn't know for sure why the open hostility of her people suddenly changed to bringing her gifts—twice in the past week—but she had a strong feeling that it had something to do with Raim's departure.

The thought of him resonated painfully in her heart.

Shoving the door aside, she brought the basket in and set it on the table. Even being here, in her own home, no longer felt the same. Whenever she turned around, she still half-expected to see Raim sitting there, gazing at her with his one good eye the colour of ice in the river in the winter.

His scent still lingered on her pillow. The curved sword of his hung on the hook by the door. And his amulet was around her neck. It had lost its wondrous glow now, dull and listless like a piece of amber she once saw someone bring to the market from the far north.

She should have tossed all Raim's things into the creek the moment she realized he had left. But she kept them, used them, wore them, as if through them she could bring him closer even if he was no longer with her.

Not wanting to stay another minute inside the cabin she had shared with Raim, Olyena packed some of the bread and sausage, putting the rest of the food away. She then grabbed his sword, slinging it over her shoulder. Both strong and elegant, the weapon reminded her of Raim even more than the amulet. Having it on her brought some of the sense of security she used to have when Raim was around.

Her gaze falling on the empty basket, she grabbed it before walking out of the door.

One never knew what walking in the woods would bring. Maybe she would find some spring onions, or the early garlic greens to fill the basket with.

SHE FOUND THE GARLIC greens on the very edge of the woods, just a few paces up the creek from the spot where she had found Raim . . .

Thinking about him again.

Yanking a small knife from under the rope she used for a belt, she bent over, resolving not to think about Raim for at least a minute.

His amulet swayed on the cord around her neck, suddenly glowing just as bright as it did when Raim wore it.

Her heart skidded to a near stop.

Was he here?

Again?

Had he come back?

Clutching the stone of the amulet in her palm, she straightened quickly, eyes scanning the area in search of Raim.

Through the underbrush behind the tree line, Olyena spotted a male figure crouching by the creek.

At first glance, the man appeared to be drinking from the stream, then she realized he was just rinsing his face and hands. His clothing was of a similar cut and material as Raim's, but the stranger's golden curls, spread on his shoulders, let her know it wasn't he.

Her hope crashed into despair and disappointment. Her knees buckling under her, she sank to the forest floor.

Possibly catching the sound of the few twigs she broke on her way down, the stranger rose to his feet promptly, turning her way.

She stilled, hoping he wouldn't see her, but he obviously had spotted her already as he was heading her way.

"Who is there?" he yelled, and she drew her head into her shoulders in an attempt to make herself smaller, wishing she could make herself invisible. Meeting a stranger in the woods rarely turned to her benefit.

"I won't harm you," he promised.

His words didn't reassure her much—a long sword dangled at his side, and a short axe was hooked to his belt.

"Who are you?" he asked, parting the underbrush between them.

Having been found, she got up to her feet, rolling her shoulders out and now wishing she was bigger.

"No matter who. Just get on your way," she said somberly.

Not quite meeting his stare, she could almost feel it slide down her body in an assessing way, although the purpose of his assessment wasn't clear yet.

"Where did you get that sword, little one?" he asked. His voice firm—curious, but not hostile.

Sword.

She quickly placed her hand on its pommel, feeling a little more confident about the situation.

"I know how to use it," she warned.

"Where is the man who owned it?"

"He is not a man," she replied gruffly. Another quick glance at the amulet on her chest revealed it burned brighter than ever. "Just like you are not, either."

"So, you've met Raim?" The stranger tilted his head to the side, staring at the pendant, too. "Can you tell me where he is then?"

'I wish I knew that myself.' She sighed inwardly.

"What do you want with him?" No matter where he was, Olyena wished no ill for Raim. If this demon was his enemy, she was not inclined to give him any information whatsoever.

"I'm his partner. His friend." He took a step back and lowered his head in a formal bow, before introducing himself, "My name is Gremory. Raim and I had been travelling together when we were attacked and separated. He didn't mention me?"

"No." Olyena hadn't asked for many details about Raim's life. When he was with her, she was happy being in the bubble of the moment with him. Nothing else mattered then.

Gremory nodded, visibly confused. "Normally, he would be searching for me."

"He was hurt." She felt the need to defend Raim.

"So was I. It took me weeks to recover, and I've been tracking him ever since."

"You've been following him?"

"Yes. It's not that hard to track Raim." Gremory huffed a humourless laugh. "One just needs to follow the trail of corpses and mutilated men."

He took another close look at her, and she recognized the intensity in his stare. Raim often gazed at her like that, as if searching for something deep inside her very soul. The longing for him painfully twisted her insides.

"He . . . left," she said softly, blinking away the tears that suddenly swelled in her eyes.

"Did he hurt you in any way?" Gremory's eyebrows, the colour of ancient gold, furrowed into a frown. The concern in his voice proved to be more difficult to bear than any hostility. It disarmed her.

Leaning back against a young birch tree for support, she brushed off an errant tear.

"No. He didn't harm me." She flinched under his examining gaze. It felt as if he already knew the truth, no matter what she said.

"Not in the way he hurt the others then." Gremory nodded, with a knowing look. "Listen . . . Is that your basket?" He picked it up and offered her his hand to help her out into the clearing. "How about I walk you back to the village, and you will tell me everything. Specifically, I'd love to know how you came into the possession of the sword and the amulet. Raim has never parted with either. Then maybe you can point me in the direction he went."

"I don't live in the village," Olyena sniffled. She straightened the vest over her shirt, pulling herself together. With one cautious glance at his outstretched hand, she took it, getting some comfort from the strength she felt in him when she leaned on it.

"I'll take you to whatever place you call home then."

Chapter 16

RAIM, THE GRAND MASTER—months after having won the position, he still loved the sound of it. It stoked something inside him, giving him a feeling of immense satisfaction he had never felt before. Only once during his existence had he felt something stronger than that. And that was in the small cabin in the woods.

The memories of it—of her—never stopped haunting him, but he forced himself to focus on the many tasks he had at hand now.

With the help of Stolas, Raim made lists of the names of every Incubus in this world. He then put a process in place to update the list regularly, to track the whereabouts of each and every one of them.

Being out there held its dangers, the close contact between demons and humans had often proved hazardous for both. And Raim wanted to know where each Incubus was at any given time. If any one of them was injured or fell into Deep Sleep, a team was dispatched to retrieve him and bring him back to the Base where he could then recover in peace.

Very few of the Incubi managed consistently to keep their self-control around humans and their precious emotions. People died as a result of running into an Incubus. Demons often ended up wounded and hurt. Also, Raim now knew firsthand about how easily the control of an Incubus could slip away when faced with the sweet smile of a woman.

To keep both races safe, a greater divide between them was needed.

Raim demanded that Incubi spend more time at the Base, rather than feeding freely outside. The teams of those with better control were encouraged to bring in whatever Sources they encountered outside, to feed the rest of the demons at the Base.

With their freedoms diminishing, many demons had opposed his changes. Raim dealt with those quickly and ruthlessly, starving them until they fell into Deep Sleep or by exiling them to the place between the dimensions—Inferno—for a few decades. Removing the disobedient ones allowed him to establish better control over the rest.

He streamlined whatever laws the Incubi had, adding a number of new rules and increasing the punishments for disobedience. Those who actively protested were also banished to Inferno.

'All of this is ultimately for their own good,' he told himself to dissuade the guilt and doubts.

Still, the most important part of his plan had not been implemented. Raim had not acted on his initial idea of Incubi taking over this world and enslaving humans.

Forcing the mortals to become nothing more but Incubi food sources no longer seemed acceptable. He didn't dare to analyze the reasons for that in depth, knowing they would have a lot to do with the woman he left alone in the woods.

Raim had tasted her fear and despair in the aftermath of being mistreated by her own kind and he couldn't bring himself to order the same treatment be done to other women.

This was more proof that being with her had weakened him.

She was the reason he had abandoned the plans of domination.

His ruthlessness, his decisiveness, his very confidence—all were affected after he had spent time in close proximity with a human woman.

Walking into the meeting room at the Base one night, Raim laid eyes on the female Source who was already sitting on the silk floor cushions there. One of the retrieval teams had brought her in. She had been fed a good meal, given a bath and some new clothes, and was now patiently awaiting being used for a Feeding.

Taking a seat on one of the several cushions at the opposite wall, Raim joined other Council members then gave a signal to the Incubus standing next to the woman to proceed. The demon had been carefully selected by Raim from a group of those who could control their hunger better around humans.

"Will it be all of you?" the woman asked the Incubus, nervously sweeping the room full of Incubi with her gaze.

"No," the demon replied. "I'll be the only one touching you. The rest will just watch if you don't mind."

The woman released a breath, relief spreading through her like a cool, milky tide. But it was the warm glow of gratitude that lit inside her at hearing the comforting voice of the Incubus that raised the alarm in Raim.

"Silence!" he ordered firmly.

The Incubus shot him a puzzled glance but obeyed, wordlessly sliding the silk caftan off the woman's shoulders.

Her skin was much darker than Olyena's, Raim noted, almost as dark as his own. Her long hair had a wave to it. But the ink-black colour of her tresses and the way some of them had fallen over her face—making his fingers itch with the desire to brush them aside—sharpened the image of Olyena in his mind.

He closed his eyes for a moment, struggling to collect himself. At the sound of the woman's gasp, followed by a soft moan, he opened them again. The hand of the Incubus was cupping the woman's breast, her dark nipple poking from between his fingers.

The warm, silky sensation of Olyena's skin under his palm came to Raim's mind, bringing with it the longing for that moment and the memory of the deep satisfaction and comfort he only ever felt when he was with her.

Unable to tear his gaze away from the male hand massaging the woman's breast, he fought a feeling of unease. The contact didn't feel right—too much risk for the Incubus taking what he shouldn't. Too close a connection between the two.

How could Raim completely trust the self-control of any demons, if he had his own tested severely by close contact with a human woman?

Ripping his riding gloves from under his belt, Raim tossed them at the Incubus.

"Put these on," he bit out sharply.

Making the Incubi wear gloves while pleasuring the Source during the Feeding would increase the number of demons he could assign this task to, he told himself. It was merely a practical solution, after all.

The dark pink wave of the woman's arousal reached him, and he skimmed it quickly.

It was good.

Nourishing and tempting . . .

And it was different enough from the taste of the one he needed to forget.

FORGETTING DIDN'T PROVE to be easy.

Months went by, but time brought no peace to the new Grand Master. In addition to the memories of Olyena that would not let him be, the worry for Gremory, who still had not return to the Base after more than a year now, had been steadily growing stronger.

Raim had never spent this much time without knowing Gremory's whereabouts. Almost all of the Incubi under his command had been accounted for, except for his very own partner, the second half of his team. And Raim was the last one who saw him.

The teams Raim had sent in search of Gremory had all returned empty-handed, there wasn't even a trail to follow. He feared the worse, his partner had either been severely, repeatedly injured, which physical-ly prevented him from returning to the Base, or he had run out of energy and fallen into Deep Sleep in some remote area where no human had come to wake him up.

Either way, Gremory needed help. And since no one Raim had sent was able to locate him, he headed back up north himself.

Guilt urged him to hurry as he travelled. If Gremory had indeed been stopped by a grave injury, if he lay tortured by Deep Sleep somewhere, then it should have been Raim's priority to find and help him as soon after their separation as possible. Instead, he spent that time in Olyena's arms.

The pull of the memories of her grew more powerful the closer he came to the area where she lived, as if the invisible string that she had connected herself to him grew stronger, drawing him in. So strong, that he took the turn towards her cabin as soon as he reached her woods.

His heart raced wildly as he approached the small clearing where her cabin stood. Any caution left him when he spotted the tiny structure through trees. He stepped into the clearing, leading his horse by the reins behind him.

With a knock on the door, he opened it, expecting to be greeted by the warm smell of cooking and the sight of Olyena's small frame. Anticipation had taken over, making nothing else matter. If she called to him again, he'd stay. He would surrender and forget everything else.

But the place was empty when he opened the door. Not in a way that meant the occupant had just stepped out for the day, but that she had been gone for a long time now—weeks, maybe months—with no obvious intention to return.

The shutters had been left open, anything of any value gone. There hadn't been fire made in the stove for a while—mushrooms were growing in it. The packed dirt floor was littered with old leaves and debris. No sound from the chicken coup certainly meant that the chickens were gone, too.

A sharp lance of disappointment shot through Raim, then an alarm rose inside him. Quickly, he searched for any signs of struggle or violence that might have driven Olyena to abandon her home. The place was empty, but not ransacked. Nothing was broken, even the few pieces of furniture inside weren't moved or upturned.

Still, the feeling of guilt grew heavier in his chest, weighing down on him to the point it was hard to breathe.

Leaving the cabin, Raim made it to the village by nightfall. The first peasant he accosted on the outskirts didn't recognize him, as he had long healed completely, leaving no trace of an injury on his face and no need for an eyepatch.

The villager told him that the witch's dark, scarred guardian turned into a handsome, golden-haired man over a year ago. The two of them left a few months after that, never to be seen in the forest again.

Raim spent a few long months, searching for a trail of the couple through the Kievan Rus and deeper into the volatile European parts of the continent, but to no avail.

Eventually, he had no choice but to return back to the Base in the Empire—angry, disappointed, and . . . desperately feeling the loss of the woman and the demon, the only two beings in this world he had ever allowed to come close to his heart.

Chapter 17

THE HOLY ROMAN EMPIRE

15th Century

"Are you sure?" Raim leaned deeper into the shadows by the wall of the tavern, drawing the hood of his cloak lower over his face, lest the few humans lingering on the street glimpse his face.

Ever since he had moved the Council to the sleepy parts of Kievan Rus two centuries ago, he had been leaving the Base much more often than he allowed any other Incubus.

Here, in the tiny village at the foothills of the Alps, he was far away from the new Incubi Base that was now seated deep in the woods where Olyena's cabin once stood.

"Are you sure it was them?" he asked the human male again.

It had been nearly four centuries since Raim's return to the cabin when he found it abandoned. All logic told him that the couple, which this man informed him had been spotted heading for the Alps the day prior, could not be Olyena and Gremory. Being mortal, Olyena should have been long dead by now. Still, Raim had never abandoned his search. Whatever reports he received had always mentioned them both, the dark-haired woman with the golden-haired man who wouldn't leave her side.

"Yes. They were going south, to the sea. A stable hand overheard them." The male stretched his hand out, the anticipation of the promised payment beamed inside him with greed. "You may be able to catch up with them before they cross the mountains if you hurry."

Raim had been away from the Base for far too long already. Yet the temptation to keep going, now that he was this close, got even stronger.

Silently, he handed the man the payment for the information.

"Did your sweetheart leave you for another?" the human blurted out, the weight of gold in his hand making him too chatty for his own good.

A spike of rage speared through Raim. He grabbed the male by the throat.

"For a mortal, you are way too insolent," he hissed through his teeth, siphoning just enough life energy from the man to make him pass out, without killing him. "You need to take better care if you want to keep your short pathetic life a bit longer." He tossed the man under the wall.

For a demon, Raim himself had become way too sensitive, he realized bitterly.

Without sparing another glance for his informer, he headed to his horse that would take him south to the Alps.

HE HAD TO LEAVE HIS horse behind, the higher up the mountain he climbed. Traveling on horseback along the steep path was no longer possible.

Only when the sun was already partially hidden behind the mountain peaks on the horizon had the faint smell of a campfire reached him, and Raim realized he had caught up with the couple he had pursued for centuries.

Carefully watching his step so as not to lose his footing on the narrow path and launch off the cliff to the rocky valley below, Raim made his way around an outcropping between the few short, skinny trees.

The campfire was bright. Hung over it, a cast iron pot bubbled lively. Several bundles of luggage and equipment, including a couple of bedrolls and furs, lay nearby, but no one appeared to be around.

"Stop right there!" A tall figure moved from the shadows into the circle of the campfire light. Even before the glow lit his face, Raim recognized his voice.

"Gremory," he exhaled, afraid to believe his quest was finally over.

"What do you want, Raim?" The Incubus raised the curved sword in his hand.

Raim's sword.

It was made in Persia, a while before Incubi came to this world. Raim had liked its slim, curved blade—lighter than many weapons of the time when he acquired it, yet no less deadly in his hand.

What *did* he want?

During most of his search, he simply followed the drive to find them. Without Gremory, his life at the Base felt even more hollow than before, despite the high rank of his position. Questions about Olyena's fate had been tormenting him ever since he saw her abandoned dwelling.

"I want you back at the Base," he replied firmly. "Where you belong."

"I belong with her," the demon claimed.

"Olyena?"

Gremory nodded.

"How is she still alive?"

"As long as I'm with her, she doesn't die."

Impossible.

Could Olyena have truly been a witch? In possession of some power that he missed in her? Was that how she had attained her hold over him, too?

"She enthralled you . . ." Raim gasped.

"She is mine."

"No. She is human—never meant to be with either of us." His words clashed with the possessive feeling that swelled hot inside him.

Olyena was supposed to be *his*. He saw her first. He touched her first, too, taught her how to enjoy a man's attention.

The bitterness of the loss burnt even stronger at the thought that it had taken him this long to realize that. Regret was unbearable.

If he couldn't have her, no one should.

"You are an Incubus, Gremory. Your place is among us, not with her."

"There is no way back for me, Raim. I'm not like any of you. Not anymore." Lowering the sword, the demon stepped closer. "Look at me. *Really* look at me. What do you see?"

Raim did what he rarely bothered to do, he focused his attention on the feelings churning inside the Incubus. Normally, those would be just empty echoes of whatever emotions he had consumed last. But that was not what he found inside Gremory this time.

Every colour of a rainbow curled and shimmered in a magnificent light show—potent and bright.

They were no longer just *her* emotions, they belonged to both of them, having taken a life inside Gremory, too.

"I *feel*, Raim—all of this." The demon pressed his clenched fist to his chest with force. "I love her."

"You . . . what?" Raim swayed back, as if Gremory had physically hit him. His foot slipped on the rocky path, sending a shower of dirt and loose stones off the cliff and down the steep mountain side.

"I belong to her, just as she does to me—"

"She was never meant to be yours!" Raim bellowed, releasing his confusion, his longing, and his rage with this one cry of anguish.

'She should have been mine!'

Anger blinded him. The familiar feeling—aggression—could never hurt *him*. It was there to cause pain to others. And he let it take over.

Yanking the sword from the scabbard at his hip, he leaped to Gremory, who lifted Raim's old weapon in defence.

"You'll have to let us be, Raim," his old partner growled, cutting through the air with the sword aimed at Raim's neck.

Raim twisted, receiving the blow to his upper arm instead. He felt his bone crack, rendering his left arm nearly useless. Lunging forward, he struck, sinking the tip of his blade into Gremory's side, right between his ribs.

"No!" A feminine voice screamed from up the mountain. Rocks and gravel rolled down as a woman hurried to the flat ground of the campsite where the two demons fought.

Dropping the armload of dry twigs and branches she must have been collecting up the mountain, Olyena ran into the circle of campfire light.

"Gremory!" She rushed to her demon. "What has he done to you?"

Flabbergasted, Raim stared at the woman who had refused to leave his thoughts for four centuries now. She had not changed at all. Aside from different clothes, everything about her was exactly how he remembered.

The long braid, the colour of a crow's wing.

The milky-pale skin, not a single line of aging marring her face.

His tear-shaped amulet was still around her neck. She must have kept it for protection against the likes of him.

The fire of resentment that burned in her dark eyes when she glared at him was new, though.

"Olyena . . ." He could almost taste her name on his tongue, saying it out loud for the first time in so many years.

"Go away, Raim!" she tossed his way, supporting Gremory, who swayed on his feet. The blood from his wound dripped steadily between his fingers and onto the ground.

"I didn't even break his rib," Raim muttered, getting more confused—a wound like that, even as deep as Raim had made it, wouldn't stop a demon. The loss of blood would never slow him down, either.

I'm not like any of you.

A sudden realization hit him harder than any weapon ever could.

"Is he like you now?" He stared at Olyena, who took the sword from Gremory's hand. "Did you make him mortal, witch?"

"*Witch?*" she scoffed, raising the sword. "But I am just a woman, Raim. You said it yourself, witchcraft is simply a product of human imagination. Gremory may not be exactly like me, but he has never been like you, either. Unlike you, he feels. He cares. And he loves." With a strangled groan, she lifted the sword over her head. "I won't let you hurt him!" She threw herself at him.

Startled, he didn't even attempt to defend himself, taking the blow right across his chest. The force of the impact wasn't nearly as strong as Gremory's. Raim barely moved his foot back for a better balance but lost his footing on the rocky, slanted path. Before he could fully regain his balance, Olyena struck again, this time stabbing straight through his chest and knocking him off his feet.

Rolling off the path, Raim managed to get a grip on a rock protruding at the edge of the cliff, and catch a bunch of thick roots with his other hand, despite the burning pain in the cracked bone of his arm.

Hanging over the cliff, his legs dangling with nothing but the void under his feet, he stared at the woman standing above him.

Backlit by the vivid glow of the setting sun, with burning determination in her dark eyes—Olyena looked like a goddess to him. Sword raised high above her head again, thick braid draped over her shoulder, a few long strands caught by the wind flying around her face, she did not waver.

She was no longer a timid girl hiding in the woods from every living soul. She was a real woman, defending the one she loved.

"I would have made you the Grand Mistress of all of my kind," he said in awe.

"Why would I want to be your Grand Mistress, Raim? I am Gremory's *everything.*" She stepped closer, shaking her head. "I can't let you hurt him. Stop following us."

She lowered the sword, hacking off the roots he was holding on to. His injured arm lost purchase on the stone he tried to cling to, sending him off the cliff and into the darkness of the abyss below.

Chapter 18

THE BLISSFUL OBLIVION did not last long.

When Raim opened his eyes, it was deep in the night. The darkness surrounded him, broken only by the twinkle of the distant stars, high above.

He vaguely remembered the fall, the painful blows against the sharp rocks of the mountainside. Then the agony of his many injuries flooded his awareness.

Attempting to move, he realized that most of the bones in his body must have been broken—he could not lift a limb. The massive headache, as if his brain was about to explode, let him know that his skull must have been crushed, too.

Motionless, all he could do now was to lay still, waiting for his bones to heal while convulsions of excruciating pain rocked through his broken body.

Day came, then another night fell over the ravine.

The soft padding of paws on the rocky floor, followed by low growls, alerted Raim to approaching animals.

Wolves.

Their teeth sank into his muscles, ripping apart the flesh that had barely begun to knit together in the long healing process.

"Go away!" he attempted to yell at them, but his voice came out as a bubbling hiss, scaring no one. The pack stepped back a little, promptly returning, to feast on his body again when they realized he was unable to do much more than that.

The wolves left at sunrise, but he could be sure they would return. Any healing progress his bones and muscles would achieve during the day was threatened to be undone at night.

Unless someone found him, that was all he had ahead of him—excruciating, never-ending pain with no hope of healing completely, until Deep Sleep would eventually plunge him into an ocean of eternal pain.

The agony of his situation hurt even more if he thought back to how he got here. Rejected by both the only woman he had ever felt anything for and the demon whom he had trusted the most.

They both betrayed him.

Where would they be now as he lay here, no longer fully alive but never completely dead, either? Olyena and Gremory had probably descended the mountains and were well on their way to the warm waters of the Mediterranean. Neither of them most likely spared a thought about him—discarded and forgotten.

Envy for the two of them and for what they shared burned like acid, breeding the all-consuming anger that engulfed his entire soul.

The longer Raim spent in that ravine, burned by the sun during the day and devoured by wolves during the night, the more rage was becoming the only emotion in his heart, banishing all others.

He wished to never feel anything else, but rage.

"YOU'RE STILL ALIVE, aren't you?" The female voice rang with mild curiosity, completely devoid of any fear or disgust that could have been expected in a human at the sight of him, now.

After another nightly visit by a pack of wolves, Raim no longer had eyes to open. He couldn't see, but he listened carefully.

"Hmm. This is highly unusual for this world," the voice continued. Then Raim felt a poke in his ribs, probably with the toe of a boot or maybe with a stick. "A human would never survive in this state—they are so pathetically fragile."

He heard a rustle of skirts as the woman speaking must have crouched at his side.

"You aren't human," she concluded with an insight that was above that of regular people. "Not one of us, either, because I sense that you're a male, although there isn't much left of you for me to tell for sure, to be honest. You must be one of those who have been banished to this world? An Incubus? I've heard of you, but have never seen one with my own eyes until now."

Raim felt a vague sensation of touch to his chest, or whatever had remained of it now. He attempted to say something, ask for help, but only some coarse hissing came out.

"You are in terrible shape, honey." Despite her using the term of endearment, her voice remained neutral, no warmth of emotion filtered into it, no compassion either. "If I leave you here, you may end up rotting for decades, if not centuries. People normally use the pathway higher up the mountain to cross. I only came down here, because the passage is too steep for my horse and I can carry enough water for him, since I don't need any myself. But I may have a use for you. If you agree to help me, I'll get you out of here."

Anything.

Raim would do whatever she wanted if she helped him leave this place. He tried to voice his agreement, but to no avail once again.

"Don't bother with words—your throat is ripped out, you won't be able to make any intelligible sound, anyway. Just keep quiet if you agree. There is a small male monastery a few days walk from here. They won't let a woman anywhere near, of course. I was planning to sneak in at night, but if I have a male companion, I will be allowed to camp outside their walls, without question. With any luck, I'll get a monk or two to visit me through the night—we both will get fed. I'm starving. I'm sure you are, too."

He kept quiet, just as she told him to, to signal his agreement.

"Wonderful then." She straightened up, judging by the sound and the direction of her voice. "We'll camp there for a week or two, so you can heal a little. Then I'm heading south to Genoa, maybe to Venice after that. Both are more civilized places than the north, I must say. I'm searching for somewhere where people take their time to enjoy the finer things in life, including sex."

More sounds followed, then Raim felt the weight of a blanket or an animal hide on him as she wrapped his mutilated body in it.

"I am a Succubus, by the way. Not sure if you've heard of us. There are only a few of our kind in this world. I go by many names, but you can call me Caryss—whenever you have healed enough to speak again, that is."

She lifted Raim up easily then placed him on the top of her saddle. The horse snorted loudly and shifted under the gory burden his mistress was forcing it to carry.

"Shhh. You'll get fed, too. You may even get some oats from the good old monks," Caryss calmed the animal down, petting it on the neck and starting it on its way. Walking alongside the horse, she gave Raim a small pat through the blanket, too. "Let's go, Incubus. If our arrangement works, I may keep you around for as long as it takes for you to recover completely. I find it definitely more convenient to travel with a male companion in this world. It would be nice for a change to have one I won't be tempted to drain whenever I feel peckish."

Chapter 19

IT TOOK RAIM WEEKS before he could talk and walk again, months until he looked and felt fully himself. On the outside.

Inside, Raim never felt the same again.

Ever.

It was as if any ability to feel anything at all either had rotted out of him on that ravine floor, or been carried away by the wolves.

While healing, Raim travelled to Genoa with Caryss, and from there to Venice. He played the role of her companion whenever it was convenient for her, and left her one on one with her victims whenever she was feeding.

He sustained himself by skimming whatever positive emotions he could gather while walking through the crowded streets or visiting local markets. The very thought of touching a female body in any intimate way unsettled him. For a while, even the possibility of running into Olyena by accident disturbed him greatly.

By the time he fully healed, Caryss had grown tired of both Genoa and Venice. She took a boat across the sea to Constantinople, and Raim headed back to the Incubi Base.

For a while, his life seemed to regain its balance after he resumed his regular activities. As their Grand Master, protecting his kind was supposed to be his priority. He believed he was looking after their interests, and it gave his existence a purpose.

When he had moved the Base to Eastern Europe, Raim convinced everyone on the Council, including himself, that the change was solely for the benefit of all Incubi. The new site was remote and far less populated than many other parts of Europe or Asia. Yet human Sources were still available in quantity sufficient to maintain the Incubi feeding schedule he had established.

No matter what he told himself, though, he couldn't stop the restless feeling that fluttered through his insides when he walked through the woods outside of the Base. Almost daily, he went to the spot where he first met Olyena, watching the water run in the creek.

The small cabin in the woods was long gone of course, every single log had rotted into the ground over the centuries.

The small village—the home of Olyena's tormentors and the site of Raim's carnage—had vanished also. The whole area was now a part of the Grand Duchy of Lithuania, which was not much more than another name for Incubi. What mattered was that another settlement nearby, named Minsk, had grown in size, big enough to sustain hundreds of Incubi, but still remote enough from the world's most populated and volatile areas to keep any unwanted interest away from the Base.

Throughout the centuries that followed, Raim resumed his obsessive tracking of Olyena and her demon.

Both had told him not to follow them, but neither of them ever left his thoughts. For Raim, keeping track of their whereabouts remained the only way to still have some connection with them, though he would never admit that.

Reports came infrequently but fairly regularly. Through them, Raim knew that Gremory had recovered from his injury. He and Olyena continued to travel through Europe, staying in any one place for a few decades at a time only. Obviously needing to conceal their enduring youth and extended lifespans, they never remained in an area for longer than that.

Around the start of the seventeen hundreds, a report came that the two of them left on a ship sailing across the Atlantic to the New World.

Instead of the relief that Raim hoped to feel at having an entire ocean separate him from those who betrayed him, an agonizing sensation of loneliness crushed him at the news.

He barely made it without so much as a word about either Gremory or Olyena for a few decades. After that, he gave in to his obsession and devised a plan to split the Council in two—one for each hemisphere.

Politically, it made sense at that point. Although the population of the Western Hemisphere grew steadily, there were still many remote areas in both Americas for a new site for the Base. A second Council was formed, and Raim moved it to the New World.

He had kept his quest a secret from other Incubi, but constantly recruited a number of humans to track the couple who had been his focus and obsession for most of his existence.

For decades, there was nothing. Then, in the eighteen hundreds, a report came that caught his attention.

"You said you don't have their description," Raim flexed his jaw muscles, getting irritated with the man he'd paid a decent amount of money to, yet who so far had failed in delivering any useful details.

Raim had travelled quite a way south from the Base, a journey that took him weeks, to meet with this human contact.

"Not a *physical* description," the man corrected. "But the two who were detained in Dunvall Town have been accused of witchcraft."

"To my knowledge," Raim retorted coolly, "there have been quite a few people accused of witchcraft during the past few centuries, both in the old and the new world. What makes you think these two are the couple I'm searching for?"

"The woman is a *real* witch," the man hurriedly protested. "With her help, her lover can lift things ten times his weight. He walked through a solid rock wall once, too. There were witnesses . . ."

"He did that?" Raim's hope spiked. His gold might not be wasted yet.

"Yes," the man rushed, spurred by Raim's interest. "When they first brought them in, he tried to escape. A number of respected town folks testified seeing him disappear into the wall, like an apparition. Likely, some of the sheriff's people were on the other side at that time, questioning his woman. They called reinforcements and managed to detain him again, but he killed and injured a number of folks during the ordeal. There are murder charges against him too, now."

The information was enough for Raim to head further south, to the small, dusty settlement, called Dunvall Town. Though, he had only the vaguest idea of what he would do once he got there. Despite his fixation on tracking the two, he had no intention of confronting the couple again.

Both Gremory and Olyena had made it clear that night in the Alps that neither of them wanted to have anything to do with Raim. The pain of that rejection was still fresh in his chest, and he had no desire to go through that again.

Neither did Raim feel inclined to help the couple in any way, now that they had gotten themselves into trouble and obviously could use his assistance.

He should view this as karma, his way to extract revenge on them for leaving him on the bottom of the ravine in the Alps.

The fact that he stopped at the bank where the Council kept some of the Incubi money and filled his saddle bags with gold—good old gold as opposed to the flimsy paper cheques and notes that banks had started to use of late—of course did not mean that Raim was rushing down south to buy the freedom of those who had betrayed him.

Chapter 20

"WHAT DO YOU MEAN BY *relocated*?" Raim gripped the door-frame of the entrance to the local courthouse where he had been directed to for information on the couple he believed to be Gremory and Olyena. The wood made a creaking noise, forcing him to release his grip, lest the broken frame catch the attention of the sheriff's office employee. Raim felt too irritated already to deal with any further delays that might cause.

"I mean the two accused you're inquiring about were transferred by wagon to Lintonvale," the man replied huffily. "The holding cell there is in the basement, and it was deemed better suited to contain the male prisoner."

"When?"

"This morning." The arrogant male gave Raim a measuring stare, noticing without a doubt the dirt of the road on his boots and coat, not to mention his general dishevelled state after the days of hard travel. His last horse fell about an hour ago, forcing him to make the rest of his way here on foot.

"I need a horse." Raim ignored the man's stare, producing a few coins from the bag over his shoulder.

"Well," the official adjusted his jacket, tossing a suspicious glance at the gold Raim deposited on the stand by the door. "I would advise you to inquire at the saloon at the end of the main street. They do have some for sale, occasionally—"

"Whose horse is tied right here, outside of the court house?" Raim interrupted impatiently.

"That would be mine—"

"Great." Raim turned to leave.

"It's not for sale, though . . ." the official hurried behind him, but Raim no longer paid any attention to him.

Time was pressing. The wagon he had to catch might have made it all the way to Lintonvale by now.

HE FOUND AN UPTURNED wagon on the side of the road, a few hours East from Dunvall Town. The signs of a struggle around it appeared fresh. The bodies of the officials who must have been those accompanying the prisoners were still warm when he checked. A wide trail of footprints led away from the site of the crash.

Hope warred with worry in Raim as he steered his horse off the road and into the hills surrounding it, following the messy path of several sets of footprints intermingling with prints of horses' hooves.

Did Gremory manage to overpower his captors and free himself and Olyena? Or did someone else intercept the wagon?

The smell of smoke reached his nostrils, making Raim believe he was approaching a campsite at first. Only after cresting the next hill did he realize what was ahead of him.

A wood pyre.

The one that humans used to burn their dead throughout their history. Or to bring a capital punishment to those accused of witchcraft . .
.

Just a couple of centuries ago these were more common, both in the old and the new world. As humanity grew, people had been progressing in many ways, leading Raim to believe they had moved past the nonsense of burning their own kind at the stake by now.

But there it was.

A pyre, with two long poles inserted in the middle and a figure chained to each of them.

Gremory and Olyena.

They were surrounded by a group of men—one still with a lit torch in his hands, another with a book that he was reading out loud from. A dozen or two of others stood around in a semi-circle, watching their two victims burn.

Spurring his horse on like a mad man, Raim dashed towards the raging fire at full gallop, feeling nothing but an intense urgency to get there in time.

Neither of the two looked the way he remembered. Olyena's long braid had lost its inky colour, turning silver grey, instead. Gremory's previously golden curls where now the pale shade of desert sand. Both of their faces now had the signs of aging.

Gremory's shirt was soaked in blood in the front—he had been stabbed or shot, repeatedly. Was that how they finally overpowered him?

A bullet wouldn't stop a demon. But Gremory was no longer a true demon, was he? The shots fired at him must have weakened him.

The fire rose higher. Gremory lifted his face to the sky with a deep growl of pain. Olyena's face was turned to him, her head tilted to the side, but her eyes were closed. A peaceful smile curved her lips.

Getting closer, Raim noticed that Olyena's hand was clutched in Gremory's. Then he understood the serenity of her expression, with a chilling certainty—she was already dead. Gremory had drained her to spare his beloved the suffering of burning alive. She died with a smile on her lips, giving him her lifeforce.

Raim's gaze crossed with Gremory's as he approached, wildly spurring on his horse.

The demon's chest rose and fell in shallow breaths, the choking smoke leading to a bout of violent coughing, but he did not appear afraid. Raim saw the confidence on Gremory's face, the ready acceptance of his fate. There was no fear.

A human would have already succumbed to the pain. But Raim knew that burning in a raging fire was nothing new to Gremory. The pain of hunger was harder to bear, and Raim himself went through that daily.

Unlike Gremory, however, Raim felt dark, thick horror engulf him the moment the flame fully claimed the two bodies on the pyre.

The permanence of death terrified him.

Crashing into him like freezing squall, terror set off the rage Raim always carried inside.

He was angry with himself for getting here too late. He was mad at Gremory for letting all of this happen. He was furious with Olyena for choosing Gremory over him, when Raim surely would have kept her safe.

But most of all, he was mad at himself for ever letting her go . . .

Reaching the pyre, he took his anger out on the pathetic humans who stared at him in bewilderment when he trampled the first one of them with his horse. Snatching the still lit torch from the hand of the other, he shoved it into his face, sending him to the ground in screams of pain.

Someone shot at him, hitting his horse instead. Leaping out of the saddle before he could be crushed by the wounded animal, Raim grabbed the rifle out of the shooter's hands, breaking it over the human's head and smashing his skull to pieces.

The rest blurred into messy, bloody carnage, filled with his rage, his pain, and the screams of the dying.

He maimed and killed until there was no one left—just the two charred corpses, still upright, chained to the poles amidst the dying flames.

Kicking the glowing logs left and right, burning his boots and legs, Raim made his way to them.

Charred and burned, there was nothing left of their appearance that Raim could recognize. Only the images of them in his mind and his memories were all that remained.

Desperately, he searched inside for any trace of light, hoping that their longevity might have lent them immortality. For if he were to suffer in this world for eternity, how dared they leave him here? Alone?

But there was no life left in either of them, not even in Gremory. The Incubus had traded his immortality for a woman's love.

Any trace of the beautiful light Raim saw inside the two of them that night in the Alps was now gone. They took it with them, too.

Leaving him behind.

The anguish of a complete and irreversible loss rocked through Raim, shaking his entire being. Without the blessed relief of tears, all he could do was shout at the sky in sorrow that he now knew would be the biggest curse he'd carry for the rest of eternity.

EPILOGUE

LATER, IN THE COUNCIL meeting room . . .

The woman had long, black hair, but Raim resisted closing his eyes—the images stored in his memories would appear inside his eyelids if he did, bringing more pain, anyway.

"You're so incredibly handsome," the woman murmured to the Handler who was in charge of the Feeding tonight. The Incubus remained silent, following the rules. His gloved hands fluttered along the naked body of the woman, bringing out the nourishing wave of energy.

Intercepting another heated gaze from the Source directed at the face of the Incubus fondling her, Raim noted a familiar warm tint curl through the red of her arousal. Somehow the exchange between the two had already grown deeper than it should have been between two complete strangers. And now, he was allowing it to grow even more, right here, in the Council's meeting room.

The danger of another Incubus falling into the sweet trap of a woman was evident.

Raim would need to find ways to prevent any real connection between them from ever happening.

A blindfold would help.

What a woman couldn't see, she would not be able to admire. Or Raim could find a way to cover the face of the Incubus. With a mask? Or a helmet?

Things had changed. Raim had been forced to sign the treaty with The Priory, who were in charge of the Incubi food supply ever since.

However, Raim had fought hard to remain a Grand Master, making sure to win every single election for centuries. He managed to keep control over the Incubi way of life. Therefore, he could still protect those who were awake from falling into the trap of a human woman that would ultimately lead to their demise.

He still hoped to spare others the agony of the excruciating loss and regret that he could not escape himself.

Watching the Handler reap an orgasm out of the Source, Raim skimmed her energy. He needed to feed, to remember. Hunger stripped an Incubus of his memories, but they were all Raim had left. Torturous, as they were, he hated and treasured them all.

For a demon, emotions were to feed on, he told himself, not to experience. And he crushed them all down, striving to feel nothing.

Only when he remembered, he allowed himself to feel.

The Last Unforgiven – Freed

Demons, book 5

Chapter 1

(Unedited and subject to change)

RAIM

The last symphony ended, the needle of the gramophone uselessly skipping at the edge of the record disk.

Hand on the window frame, Raim leaned his forehead against the cool glass, the night outside completely dark in the Swiss countryside, just south of the mountainous border with Austria.

A sudden loud knock on the heavy front door of his estate home scraped against his nerves. He didn't move from his position by the window, though—a demon would enter, even with the doors closed. A human could go back to wherever they came from, for all he cared.

The knock came again. Loud and persistent. As if the uninvited visitor had the right to demand the entry into Raim's house.

Letting go of the window frame, he strolled to the front door, just the way he was—shirtless and barefoot, wearing but the pair of silk pants. The intruder on his privacy would have to deal with his half-undressed state.

He opened the door. "Father?" Shocked, Raim stared at the elderly man who was flanked by two younger humans in suits. He had met the current Priory Elder on many occasions, but never had The Elder personally visited Raim in any of his dwellings.

Until now.

The large black vehicle was parked on the circular driveway. Served Raim right for neglecting locking the gate.

"To what curse of the Devine do I owe the honour of your visit?" Raim asked flatly, not inviting The Elder in.

"I need to talk. Coming here myself seemed like a more practical option to the summons of you." The man held Raim's stare with challenge.

The memories of the burning lashes of chants as his demonic essence hovered suspended in the power of a summoner creeped hot and cold up Raim's spine.

The Elder could not remember any of that because he wasn't there—couldn't have been—Raim's summons happened more than six hundred years ago. Many generations and many Elders had changed since. However, humans had long found a way to preserve their knowledge through records and archives, way past their limited lifespans.

The Elder was not even born then, but he knew all about Raim's disgrace. And he never failed to remind him of the one and only time Raim had fully submitted to a human.

"Let me come in," the old man demanded.

"What for? I'm no longer a Grand Master and have no business with your Priory."

"So I've heard. You've abdicated your position."

"Abdicated?" Raim scoffed. "It wasn't a royal throne."

"Maybe, but you have reigned—"

"Not anymore," he bit out, The Elder was beginning to test his patience. If it wasn't for the plain curiosity about the purpose of his visit, Raim would have shut the heavy door in his face already.

"You are The Grand Master, Raim," The Elder stated, mater-of-fact. "Always have, always will be."

Raim drew in a long inhale. In a way, the human was right. As the only Incubus who had never spent a day in Deep Sleep, Raim had been awake and alert all his life, a witness and a participant of every event pertinent to Incubi's existence in this world. The title of Grand Master that he had fought so hard to gain and keep had become a part of him, he no longer could be completely rid of it even after giving it up.

"Why are you here?" Raim scanned the man's emotions quickly. His unusually genuine serenity was puzzling. The strong mistrust and hostility Raim normally saw in members of The Priory was muted by confidence in The Elder this time, instead of being amplified by fear as it often was.

"I've come to have a chat with an old friend." The Elder slid the end of his walking stick in the gap between the door and the frame, obvious about gaining the entry.

"Friend?" Raim lifted his eyebrow in question. The desire to find out the true purpose of this visit, finally, made him open the door wider. The Elder entered promptly, leaving his escort outside. "You must truly believe in our 'friendship' if you are willing to come in alone," Raim commented. "Either that, or you're losing your common sense, old man."

"My common sense tells me that if you wanted to harm me, my bodyguards wouldn't be able to stop you, anyway. They may as well stay outside."

Raim spotted a sliver of orange glow between the buttons of The Elder's suit jacket—the man was wearing his *soros* amulet. He did not entirely place his safety in Raim's hands, after all.

"Very well then." Instead of going back to the sitting room with the gramophone, Raim led The Elder to the more formal and less intimate grand room of the house, making sure to enter it first. It would be ridiculous to let The Elder's amulet lock him out of a room in his own house, leaving him having to request a permission to enter it afterwards.

"Can I offer you a drink?" he asked, playing the part of a host.

"Do you have anything older than me?" The teasing glimmer in The Elder's eyes reflected his good humour, again making Raim wonder about the reasons for this unexpected serenity in the man.

"Older than you? Plenty." The hatch of the antique liquor cabinet squeaked when Raim opened it, taking out the dark, dusty bottle he brought from Scotland several decades ago. "Scotch?"

"Please." Propping his walking stick against an armchair in front of the grand fireplace, The Elder lowered himself into the chair.

Pouring two crystal glasses, two fingers deep each, Raim brought one to his unexpected guest, then leaned against the mantle of the fireplace.

The Elder took a tiny sip from the glass and closed his eyes, obviously savoring the drink. His expression brought to Raim's mind the faces of the Council members during the Feedings, when they consumed the sexual energy of the human Sources, savoring every drop of it.

"This bottle could fetch thousands of euros today," the man observed, staring through the whisky in his glass at the light of the chandelier.

"Maybe, if I had any intentions of selling it." Raim took a sip of the amber liquid himself.

Normally, he preferred the taste of wine to any hard liquor. Wine gave him the illusion of relaxation. The intense burn of the nearly-century-old whisky right now was more fitting, though. There was nothing relaxing about dealing with The Priory.

"Why are you here?" he repeated, keeping The Elder's emotions in focus.

The man set the glass on the side table, leaning back in his chair.

"In a way, I've come to say goodbye."

Another goodbye?

Not that parting with The Elder brought up the same emotions as saying goodbye to Caryss did. In fact, as far as The Elder was concerned, Raim had hardly any emotions at all.

"The doctors gave me six months to live," the man continued. "Cancer . . ." He pocked at his chest with his thumb in several places, as if stubbing the tumours inside.

"I'm sorry to hear that," Raim replied evenly. All humans died. It was simply the matter of when and how.

"I've decided, however, that I won't be needing more than two of those months," The Elder added unexpectedly.

"Are you planning to end your own life?"

"My death is imminent. I am simply planning to take control of how it will happen." The Elder steepled his fingers in front of him, an odd smile playing on his face. "I've also decided to make it worthwhile by taking all of you with me."

The Elder paused, as if giving Raim some time to absorb his words.

After a moment of confusion, understanding flooded Raim, prickling his skin with cold.

"The *soros* urn."

His mind quickly flashed back to that dreadful day he was summoned by The Priory's Elder, over six hundred years ago.

The summoner was strong. That was the only time in history when an Incubus was fully brought under the power of a human. And that Incubus happened to be Raim. Completely exhausted by the futile attempts to resist, he had accepted the man as his Master. Under his orders, Raim had read and translated the carvings on the *soros* urn from the language of his world. The Priory Monks recorded their meaning for the eternity.

That day, Raim also made himself the only demon who ever escaped the bond of his Master after it had been formed. His ever-present rage proved to be stronger than the hold of the chants. The aggression exploded inside him, giving him the burst of strength to loosen the bond that held him a slave. He used that moment to kill the summoner and break the circle to escape.

No one dared to summon Raim again after that. There was no point for him to hide behind a human name either, since *his* had already been recorded for all of The Priory to know for the centuries to come.

The treaty that Raim signed with them shortly after was an attempt on the part of both parties to find a way to co-exists. However, by finding the one undamaged urn first and taking it into their possession, the members of The Priory gained an upper hand. From then on, they had the means to end Incubi's existence on Earth at any moment, simply by touching the urn.

They held this threat over Raim's head ever since.

"You're a foolish human." Raim shook his head.

"Most would consider my sacrifice heroic," The Elder argued with a pretentions air. "I will finally accomplish what no one has dared to do before—touch the *soros* urn and put an end to all Incubi on Earth.

"You will take all of your Priory with you, too." That was what the writings, engraved on the urn, warned about. The touch of a human or a demon would banish the Incubi blood from this world. Every last drop . . .

The engravings also stated that the humans responsible would perish, too.

"If you touch the urn, all of us will be gone, including every one of your precious Priory."

"Not necessarily. The carvings read 'those who touch and those in charge of the urn will vanish.'"

"Right. The Priory is in charge."

"I am The Elder of the Priory, responsible for the whole organization and therefore in charge of the urn. If I touch it—alone—I will be the only one who'll die."

"Is that what you told them?" Raim scoffed. "Is that how you've managed to convince the rest of your Brothers to back your plan?"

"My Brothers didn't need to be convinced. There are quite a few of us who believe that demons must be cleansed off the face of the Earth, no matter the cost. We've had the means to be rid of you—fully and completely—for generations. Yet, the cowards before me never used this power to do what's right."

"*'Quite a few'* doesn't mean *'all.'*" Raim noted the righteous conviction within The Elder waver at his words, proving his assumption correct. "You didn't share your plan of self-destruction with everyone, did you?"

The Elder remained silent just long enough for Raim to see the truth inside him.

"You are about to murder everyone in your organization, without the knowledge or consent of those who would lose their lives." Raim folded his arms over his chest. "Personally, you would only be giving up a few months of pain and suffering of dying the slow death yourself. And you're trying to present your plan as a noble sacrifice on your part?"

Even after a millennium of watching humans, the extent of the evil some of them where capable of astounded him.

The Elder shifted in his chair, regaining his composure.

"The results will justify the means. You and your kind are the abomination that does not belong to this world. Look at you . . ." he gestured at Raim's bare torso, a grimace of clear disdain distorted The Elder's features, making scanning his emotions unnecessary. "Beaming with youth and health. You are more than a dozen times my age, yet it is *me* who is standing at the edge of a grave. You will keep on living, never having to worry about what I'm dealing with or what I'm about to go through—"

"You wish for an eternity?" Raim huffed a bitter laugh, lifting his glass for another drink. "Are you envious of my curse, human?"

"If the curse is what made you impervious to decease and death, then—"

"Silence!" Raim slammed the glass on top of the side stand. The crystal shuttered, littering the surface with shards and spilling the priceless whiskey.

Shocked, The Elder swallowed the words Raim could not let him utter out loud.

No one, be he a friend or a foe, deserved this curse. The human was foolish enough to envy him, but Raim couldn't bear for anyone to wish for that upon themselves, in his presence. Some words when said out loud carried the consequences neither of them could predict or prevent.

Obviously, The Elder failed to understand any of it.

"I am going to change it all, demon." He straightened in his seat, glaring at Raim. "Promptly and completely."

Raim scanned his emotions carefully once again. This time the resentment was at full bloom. The Elder's undisguised hatred for Raim and all of the Incubi rose to the surface—thick and toxic.

"My initial plan was to let your Incubi earn their Forgiveness, since they all dove right into that—eager and willing. Then, once they have turned mortal, we would have exterminated them all, the way one gets rid of dangerous pests in their house. That would have taken time I no longer have, however. Besides, the assumption we've had for a while now has recently been confirmed—there is more of your blood out there, and I want them all gone."

"More of our blood?" Raim wondered if the man's sanity had partially departed him already.

"Your kind has been breeding, spreading your tainted demon blood all over our world for centuries."

"Your memory is playing tricks on you." Raim shook his head. "The first demon-human offspring is not even two years old yet. There have been a few more born since, I've heard, but all are still infants. Are you afraid of babies, Father?"

"They won't be babies forever, but they will live for centuries. Merging two worlds by breeding apparently gives the offspring abilities impossible to predict and therefore even harder to control for us than your kind."

"How do you know that? It's your fear that speaks in you—"

"One of our own had strayed from the principles of The Priory. He created a separate, unsanctioned by us organization, all members of which are now dead, including its founder—Monk Steffen Keller. We have been conducting an extensive investigation into his dealings and operations. He had a supplier in Toronto, Canada, whose warehouse perished in a fire over a year ago, under unexplained circumstances."

The Elder paused to catch his breath, his illness more apparent now in the rapid rise and fall of his chest and the sweat beading on his pale forehead.

"I can't say I'm sorry, either about the death of your Monk or the loss of that warehouse," Raim stated coolly.

"I did not expect you to be. We were unable to identify the person responsible for the fire, only that it was started by unnatural means. However, the incident prompted me to investigate closely a number of other, unexplained events that has been swept under the carpet, so to say, throughout the history. Specifically, those involving walking through walls, something your kind is capable of doing." The Elder lifted an eyebrow, as if waiting for Raim to confirm. Since the Priory had been well aware of this ability of Incubi, The Elder was probably just taking a break—talking obviously exhausted him, physically.

"Our investigation led to the discovery of Incubi offspring," he continued. "For centuries, they have been living all over the world, breeding with humans, over and over, to the point that it would be impossible to accurately identify those with the demon blood in them, now." Disgust thickened in The Elder's emotions, a feverish blush coloured his pale sunken cheeks. Hatred, as strong as passion rose in a black, gloomy bloom marring all colours inside him.

The toxic hate seemed potent enough to taint the old man's perception. Raim had walked this Earth for centuries, never did he hear anything about the demon offspring until the one born two years ago to Sytry and his woman, Alyssa.

"The *soros* stone urn, however, will kill them all with ease." Pressing his hands into the carved armrests, The Elder rose from his chair. "One touch, and all with Incubi blood in them would perish, stopping the spread of the demon plague on Earth in seconds. A human bred by a demon gives birth to a cambion—the abomination that does not belong to any world and therefore must die."

"If the Incubi offspring really existed and have bred for centuries, wouldn't their descendants be more human than demon by now?"

"Even a smidge of demon blood in them makes them no longer human," The Elder replied firmly. "They are not like us."

Raim considered for a moment what death would mean for the Incubi. Nearly all of them have been Forgiven by now. Their curse had ended. Their punishment had been completed. As mortals, they would die and meet with the Devine again. Then they would be given peace they had earned.

Not he, though.

"Why are you telling me all of this?" He asked The Elder, who stood in front of him, leaning on his walking stick for support. "Why going through the trouble of showing up here in person?"

"It was not that much of a trouble," the man waved him off. "I've heard you're back in Switzerland. It was a short enough drive."

"Why?" Raim insisted.

The Elder's pale eyes narrowed, he let his hatred slither through them.

"Because I wanted to see your face, Raim. I could not miss the moment you realize that your days in this world are numbered, that your centuries-long work of protecting your kind will be undone by a frail, dying man in seconds. But most of all, I wanted to give you the taste of mortality. So you'll know what it's like to spend whatever little time you have in fear, dreading what's to come and unable to do anything to stop it—the closest a demon would come to feeling the agony of death."

"I can simply kill you right now, and none of it will happen."

"If you do," The Elder smirked. "The cleansing will happen tomorrow morning, at sunrise. If I don't return to The Priory by then, another Brother will complete my mission by touching the *soros* urn himself. Go ahead, kill me. The choice is yours, but I know you care about your kind much more than you want me to believe. All of your Incubi have paired up by now. In two-months time, all of them would most certainly earn their Forgiveness and will die as humans do. If you kill me now and bring their end early, they will suffer in whatever Hell you have all come from, with you. In two months, you will be most certainly the last Unforgiven left."

Holding his gaze in challenge, The Elder waited. Not getting a response, he moved to the door, with a new bounce in his step, despite the cane. "I'll leave you now, Raim. So you can spend your last two months in the hell on earth I've just created for you."

"For a human, you have been rather perceptive and even wise at times, Father." Raim's words made The Elder pause on his way out. "But you are still merely a man. One thing you are terribly wrong about is that I do not fear leaving this world. The true agony of death falls not on those who go, but on those who stay. My own end does not scare me."

Raim pushed away from the wall he had been leaning on.

"Why would I cling to this world the way you do?" He advanced on The Elder, who flinched and shuffled back. "I have spent over a millennium here, with but a handful of moments worth to remember. I have watched generations of you come and go, civilizations rise and fall. Most of what I've learned about your kind disgusts me. You are a bunch of pathetic, self-aware, bloodthirsty animals, deriving pleasure in destroying each other. I'm sick of this world, repulsed by its inhabitants.

None of you deserve even the short lives that you get. Nothing and no one holds me here. So go, Father, do what you have set out to do." Raim led the way to the exit. "I will not stop you, but not because I'm afraid or because I care, but simply because you're finally offering me a way out of this filthy place you call Earth." He yanked the front door open, ignoring the startled stares of The Elder's escort on the other side. "Now, get the fuck out of my house."

HE LET THE ELDER GO, unharmed. As fed up as he was with this world, he chose to take the two months he was offered and give the others enough time to be Forgiven.

He lied when he said he didn't care. It was unnatural and difficult for Incubi to create a lie, but not impossible. After a millennium of practice, Raim had learned how to do that as convincingly as humans did.

Two months.

Should he warn the others? He decided not to, granting them the gift of blissful ignorance instead. Thinking about all of the Incubi soon being free from this world and back in the arms of the Devine filled him with lightness of relief. It was the best outcome for his race, one he hadn't even dared to dream of. All he could hope for now was that their human partners' loyalty would last for two months longer, sparing the Incubi the agony of heartache before the end. Surely, even the treacherous hearts of human women could keep their feelings in for that long. One could only hope.

Suddenly, the eternity he always thought he had, shrunk to just two miserly months. Was there really nothing he would miss from this world?

Absolutely nothing came to mind that would resonate with any hint of sadness or regret when he thought about leaving it behind. A myriad of faces of people whose paths he had crossed over the centuries rushed through his brain. Most were dead, the rest didn't matter.

Nothing and no one he would miss.

Except that something buzzed at the back of his mind. Not a person or an object, but a question—annoying with persistency of an unfinished business.

He gave his teardrop amulet of *soros* stone to Olyena in the eleventh century. Four hundred years later, he saw she was still wearing it. Yet it was not around the neck of her corpse on the execution pyre, two hundred years ago. Neither could he find it in the ashes and ambers at her feet then.

The last time he saw his amulet, it was on the chest of a human woman still living, just over two years ago, on a windy road in Rocky Mountains.

Doctor Neri, his excellent memory helpfully supplied her name.

A fierce woman with ink-black hair, gathered into a tight knot on the back of her head. Without having ever touched her, somehow Raim knew exactly how her hair would feel when running free between his fingers.

Suddenly, Raim realized what he wanted to do during his last two months on Earth—getting this one question answered.

How did Delilah Neri come into the possession of his amulet?

More by Marina Simcoe

Demons, 5-book Series
Demon Mine
The Forgotten
Grand Master
The Last Unforgiven - Cursed
The Last Unforgiven - Freed

Stand Alone Novels Set in Demons World
The Real Thing
To Love A Monster

Madame Tan's Freakshow
Call of Water – 2020

Midnight Coven Author Group
Wicked Warlock (Cursed Coven)
Tempted by Fae, Anthology. Available only until August 2020

Science-Fiction Romance
Experiment

Enduring (Valos Of Sonhadra)
My Holiday Tails - 2020
Gravity (Dark Anomaly Trilogy) – 2020/2021

About the Author

MARINA SIMCOE LOVES to write romance with characters, who may or may not be entirely human, because she firmly believes that our contemporary world could always use a little bit of the extraordinary.

She has lots of fun exploring how her out-of-this-world characters with their own beliefs, values, and aspirations fit into our every-day life.

She lives in Canada with her very own sexy demon, their three little angels, and a cat who might be the Lucifer himself.

For updates and for more illustrations of all of her books please visit Marina Simcoe Author page on Facebook or www.marinasim-coe.com.

Please Stay in Touch

Newsletter signup: http://eepurl.com/c__RGn
Readers' Group
Marina's Reading Cave www.facebook.com/groups/
621598474945014/
www.instagram.com/marinasimcoeauthor
www.marinasimcoe.com
www.facebook.com/MarinaSimcoeAuthor/
www.amazon.com/author/marinasimcoe
www.bookbub.com/profile/marina-simcoe
www.goodreads.com/MarinaSimcoe

www.ingramcontent.com/pod-product-compliance
Lightning Source LLC
Chambersburg PA
CBHW030815200726
48288CB00004B/1238